HASTA MAÑANA

HASTA MAÑANA

Carolyn Wilkerson

Five Star • Waterville, Maine

Copyright © 2003 by Carolyn Wilkerson

All rights reserved.

This novel is a work of fiction. Names, characters, places and incidents are either the product of the author's imagination, or, if real, used fictitiously.

First Edition, Second Printing

Published in 2003 in conjunction with Tekno Books and Ed Gorman.

Set in 11 pt. Plantin by Minnie B. Raven.

Printed in the United States on permanent paper.

Library of Congress Cataloging-in-Publication Data

Wilkerson, Carolyn.
    Hasta mañana / Carolyn Wilkerson.
    1st ed.   Waterville, Me. : Five Star, 2003.
      p. cm.
    ISBN 0-7862-5439-4 (hc : alk. paper)
    1. United States. Immigration Border Patrol—Fiction.
2. Women detectives—Arizona—Fiction.   3. Government investigators—Fiction.   4. Americans—Mexico—Fiction.
5. Sons—Death—Fiction.   6. Drug traffic—Fiction.
7. Arizona—Fiction.   8. Mexico—Fiction.   9. Suspense fiction.   10. Domestic fiction.   I. Title.
PS3623.I5455H37 2003
   813'.6—21   2003049085

Dedicated to the 336th Session of
the U.S. Border Patrol Academy

ACKNOWLEDGEMENTS

I wish to thank John Duncan of the U.S. Department of Homeland Security for the inspiration to write this novel; Kenneth Wright for the meticulous behind the scenes editing, Judy Carratura for checking the spelling, Sandi, Mike, Pauline, Donetta, Bettye, and Marcia for reading the first draft. I also wish to thank my agent Barry Malzberg for persevering, and you, the reader, for selecting this book.

PROLOGUE

SEPTEMBER 1997

"I believe in paying for what I get," Billy Rose declared. "I'll give you a diamond tennis bracelet if you tell me what you're thinking this very minute."

I couldn't tell him what I was thinking. I couldn't say, "Your habit of offering to buy my good graces offends me," especially since I'd lived on his generosity for so long. I couldn't tell him, "You're holding me too close, smothering me," when just a few months ago, I needed his strength to help me stand. I couldn't say to him, "If you truly love me you will let me go," when I already knew freedom to find myself would not bring me home to him. I couldn't tell Billy Rose my thoughts, so he offered to buy them for pennies, dollars, and then diamonds.

But the thing is, Billy Rose knows me so well he seems able to read my mind, thus prompting my mother to caution me, "Be careful what you think."

She added, "William Joseph is a possessive, spiteful boy. All he has to do is *think* you plan to cross him and you may as well do the deed."

If Billy Rose knows what I'm thinking today, he doesn't let on. But then he wouldn't. His way is to hold information close until he is ready to use it.

Dressed in denim shorts, hiking boots, and an oversized broadcloth shirt, I'm on my knees in my flowerbed and up to my elbows in flowerpots, mulch, and plant food. I do my best thinking this way and I think that for the first time since Shaun's death, I'm at peace. Not a final resolute peace, but a sustaining, enabling peace, which nurtures thoughts of independence I'm not ready to share with anyone. Especially Billy Rose.

Dressed head to toe in Ralph Lauren and accessorized by gold costing more than a year's rent on my Ventura, California apartment, Billy Rose is standing on my patio holding a folded up piece of paper and sipping from a bottle of Evian.

Billy Rose and I grew up together in Tucson, Arizona. I hadn't lived there for sixteen years, but he just returned from visiting his parents there. He's been my best friend and more; still I resented him disrupting my therapeutic commune with nature and ignored him.

After many failed attempts to engage me in casual conversation, he changed tactics. "I saw him yesterday," he announced.

Instead of responding, I used my bare hands to open a hole in the dark, moist, already-worked soil and dropped in an ice plant. I bought a dozen of them, a few mums, and other fall annuals yesterday at the flea market on Telephone Road. I planned to spend today, Labor Day, planting them.

"Miriam," he repeated. "I saw him."

This time Billy Rose's voice broke. This time the sharp edge to his tone cut my attention from the flowers to him. The question in my mind telegraphed to his.

"Him," he stared unblinking into my eyes, "Mexican Joe."

First my heart stopped beating, then it stampeded like a spooked herd of wild mustangs. I was glad I was kneeling on the ground or else I may have fallen to it.

HASTA MAÑANA

Billy Rose meant he had seen the man who killed Shaun, my son, *our* son.

Fresh into puberty, I learned to get high with my mother and one of her boyfriends. Then I became part of a junior high crowd that did the same, taking Billy Rose along for the ride. But the day I discovered I was pregnant, I stopped drinking and drugging and promised Father Angelo, the nuns, Mary Mother of Jesus, and everybody else I thought had any clout, I would never do it again if only they let my baby be healthy. They did and I haven't.

But my promise did not cover Shaun by extension.

The Roses raised Shaun from a baby and people came to know him as Billy Rose's younger brother. I am ashamed to admit it, but for many years I regarded Shaun that way, too. Then I grew up and my heart yielded to its genetic birthright. It pumped motherly love through my veins and I wanted my son in my life.

But it never happened. Shaun met Mexican Joe. Now Shaun is dead.

I struggled to keep my voice calm. "Where did you see him?"

"In Nogales," he said. "I saw a group of kids, you know the type, hanging out on the corner like we used to do, waiting for a delivery, and one of them said, 'There's Mexican Joe.' I turned and for the first time he was more than a name."

Billy Rose had told me about Mexican Joe about two months after Shaun's death. "To focus your anger," he had said. "So you'll stop looking in the face of every man you meet, wondering if he's the one." I had never seen Mexican Joe, and according to local police, neither had they.

Still struggling to make my voice sound natural, I asked, "He lives in Nogales?"

11

"I don't know where he lives, Miriam. No one told me anything except, 'he's back and forth.' I know this. He brings drugs across the border, gets his orders on a cell phone, and carries a big gun."

"A real *bandito*," I said, thinking I'd been weight training and kickboxing the last six months in hopes of a face-to-face encounter with my son's killer, only to discover he was a real life Mexican bandit. A professional thug who always has his guard up, one who shoots first and asks questions later. He might be too much for me to stop. Still I knew I would try, and I would have to do it alone; Billy Rose was unabashedly a lover, not a fighter. He was a gentle man with soft, innocent eyes, and his approach to getting even kept him so far in the background you might never uncover his involvement.

"As real as *banditos* get." Billy Rose sniffed. Then he wiped his eyes with the back of his hand. Sometimes I forgot that, having lived with him for fifteen-and-a-half years as a brother, he missed Shaun in a way I could never understand.

"But *La Migra* is good," Billy Rose said. "They will capture him sooner or later."

I stood, removed a clod of dirt from my knee and crushed it between my fingers. "What's *La Migra?*"

"You know, the federal agents we see at the checkpoints coming back from Mexico. They catch illegal aliens and drug smugglers. Maybe one day they will catch Mexican Joe."

"Maybe," I said, knowing full well "maybe" wasn't a word that let me rest easy.

"I picked up this information about *La Migra* when I was in Tucson." Billy Rose thrust the paper he'd held in his hand into my face. "They need agents in Nogales. Do you think I should apply?"

"Maybe."

CHAPTER ONE

JANUARY 1998

I arrived at the Federal Law Enforcement Training Center in Charleston, South Carolina early that January morning butt-tired from driving cross-country, and soul-weary from being cooped up in a car for three-and-a-half days. First things first. I stopped short of the entrance to the training center and speed-dialed a number.

"Well. I'm here," I told Marty in Rio Rico, Arizona. "It looks desolate but I won't complain."

"Why's zat?" Marty, short for Martina, asked. She'd flunked rehab six times. Now that she is terminal, the doctor lets her imbibe whatever dulls her pain.

Hoping for a modern medical miracle, I didn't accept his "sure death" prognosis and admonished her to live clean and eat healthy, but she ignored me, like I ignored her question now. "Gotta go," I said. "I'll explain later."

"Revenge is a man's job," she reminded me. "You're just a girl."

Marty could rev me from zero to irate in a nanosecond. Fine hairs on the back of my neck bristled. I choked on the compassion I'd felt for her just a second before. "Don't start with me," I blurted out, but then tempered it. "You'll thank me when Mexican Joe no longer sucks up the air decent people need to breathe."

"Thank you?" Marty hissed, amazingly lucid now.

"You're a stubborn, pig-headed asshole. You end up dead like Shaun and I'll curse you till the day I die."

I broke the connection, then flipped the vanity mirror down.

Having just driven from L.A. to Charleston, my appearance was testament to a penchant for sleeping in rest stops and taking whore's baths in gas station facilities. The last dousing was six hours back at an Exxon. I closed the vanity mirror, restarted the truck, drove to the gate, and stopped. A hand-lettered sign taped to the guard's booth read: *Remember the Maine.*

The guard looked at my sleep hungry eyes, the jungle of unkempt braids atop my head, the wrinkled blue warm-up suit, then made his call.

"Must be your first day," he said. "Domestics enter through the rear gate near housing." He reached for identification.

I wasn't dissuaded because the guard implied a woman's place at the Border Patrol Academy was cleaning up after men. And I wasn't inclined to repeat to him the political incorrectness of his conclusions as I had to Billy Rose when I told him I should apply for a job as a federal agent, not him. Even Marty, the one person I thought would be on my side, said I was making a fool's mistake.

"And you're supposed to be smarter than the rest of us," she had said.

Marty is my mother. Being clean, sober, and holding down a steady job all at the same time *is* smarter than the rest of them, but she already knew that.

"Smart people sometimes do dumb things," I told her. "But this isn't one of those times."

Now, to rebut the guard's hasty conclusion, I thrust papers proclaiming me a bona fide federal agent trainee into his outstretched hand. "Good thing we're not playing 'What's My Line.' "

He took the papers and stepped inside the booth.

While he scanned the papers, I scanned the area. Streetlights illuminated the pre-dawn horizon enough for me to see. To my left the Charleston Harbor resounded with shouts, boat horn blasts, and clanking chains, sounds evoking history book memories of slave auctions, war, and gore. To my right stood rows of dormitories once teeming with life of the Charleston Naval Base, now empty save for memories, plumbing, and rats.

Then I remembered the Maine. The *U.S.S. Maine* had sunk off the coast of Cuba, starting the Spanish-American War. Navy men may forget to come home, as my own father did, but they remembered to their graves the sinking of one of their battleships. So figure politics. A hundred years ago, the U.S. fought to keep Spain out of Cuba. Now it spends billions each year to prevent descendants of Spaniards from entering the U.S. And the Cuban government's posture adds *chiles* to the mix.

The guard ran his finger down a pre-printed list.

I sucked in salt-sea air. *Marty might be right*, I thought. This is a huge shadow for someone with such a thin profile. I'd become lightheaded before remembering size is not the key factor in casting shadows. Hell. My life had been a series of survival tests, not the kind sanctioned by Outward Bound, but I'd mastered them. I would endure this the same way, by focusing on something other than myself. This job put me one step closer to stopping Mexican Joe from doing to some other kid what he did to my Shaun and nothing would deter me. Not the grueling training regime where five or six members of each class of fifty customarily stepped down. And certainly not when I became a full-fledged agent in the field.

Once again confident all sixty-five inches and one-hundred-twenty-five pounds of me was primed for the task, I banished the renegade doubt from my mind.

The guard returned my papers and waved me through.

I looked up into his myrtle blue, silently amused eyes, and vowed that his public relations smile would be my official response to whatever this world called "Federal Agent" presented me.

I floored the truck, set low to the ground on small wheels the way Shaun had modified it. Gravel chinked off the wheel well and kicked back onto the guard's booth.

I was on a mission to kill Mexican Joe.

CHAPTER TWO

My name is Miriam Valencia. Ten months after entering the Federal Law Enforcement Training Center in Charleston, I was assigned to the Tucson Sector where I patrolled the southern U.S. border out of Nogales, Arizona. Unlike Dana Scully, the federal agent on "The X-Files," who wears designer suits and heels, I wear green fatigues, shoes akin to combat boots, and carry nearly fifty pounds of Kevlar vest, rough duty belt, radio, flashlight, baton, ammunition, and gun.

Despite my steadfast commitment not to be broken, the Academy training regime and the lack of female companionship wore my resolve thin. I was in excellent physical condition before entering the Academy, but still there were days during the hot, humid Charleston spring when I didn't think I could crawl across another inch of sand flea-infested beach, run another ten miles in the rain, or sit still while lying in wait for my prey in a mosquito-infested swamp.

During the four months of training, there were times I hungered for conversation with someone who understood completing five hundred sit-ups from the perspective of menstrual cramps. I would have gladly talked to the men about it, but their usual response to my venting was, "You're always bitching. You sound just like a girl."

Soon every joke ended with, ". . . just like a girl."

My lifelong defense had been to suck up my feelings and it served me well at the Academy. I put on blinders, studied hard, and rose to the top of my classes of Constitution and

Immigration Law, Spanish, Physical Training, Firearms, and Vehicle Pursuit. Any time I was down, I'd remember how the men looked when I bested them and that was the fuel firing my motivation.

But I didn't go into the Academy an angel and I didn't act like one while there. I admit to flaunting my substantial skills, especially the so-called "manly ones," and shot, drove, and ran with flair not required or welcomed.

Toward the end, the weapons instructor tired of me twirling my gun cowboy-style.

"Miss Valencia," he barked. "You are not a majorette. Your gun is not a baton."

Having been first to qualify as sharpshooter, I was riding pretty high in the saddle. I was also standing in front of a class impatient for me to fall hard, and probably would have applauded if thundering hooves tenderized me to pulp.

Still, having my wits about me, I stood at attention and took the dressing down like a man.

"You're as good a shooter as I have ever trained," he continued, "but you're not a sniper. You're one member of a team. You will never be alone . . ." he was saying. But I wasn't listening. He could not lecture me about being alone.

I was alone when I was born, with withdrawal symptoms from the alcohol Marty drank right up until her water broke. I was alone when my own child pushed out of my thirteen-year-old abdomen and I had to cut the cord. I was alone after Mexican Joe's drugs killed Shaun.

Having experienced the hollow coldness of alone, I knew at that moment I was as alone as I had ever been in my life.

Like so many other times in my twenty-nine years, I swallowed the would-be tears to hold back their flow. I would stomach being demoralized in front of the others but

HASTA MAÑANA

I would never let them see me cry.

Instead I focused on the sound of seagulls, the smell of harbor brine, and the feel of sand flea bites. When the weapons instructor finished, I snapped to. "Yes, Sir. I understand, Sir."

But my heart continued to beat the singular rhythm of a sniper's cadence.

The unseen target was Mexican Joe.

Now I work in Nogales, Arizona, as far south as you can travel on I-19 and still stand on American soil. Here about ninety-five percent of the twenty thousand legal residents speak Spanish and are of Mexican descent.

Located about twenty miles from my apartment in Green Valley, Nogales ascends from the southern floor of the Arizona desert to nestle in the nooks and crags on the side of Santa Cruz Mountain. Coming into downtown Nogales, you round a bend and a mountainside vista reveals beauty so intense it sometimes takes my breath away. I then look up the mountainside to see the town of Nogales in the state of Sonora, Mexico, a city of about two hundred thousand resident population and another thousand or so who lurk in the shadows of the border like marathon runners waiting to hear the starter's gun. The two Nogales were once one land, under one flag. All that physically separates them now is a fifteen-foot-high corrugated-tin barrier. But the political, economic, and social separation is as wide as the Rio Grande is long.

Nogales, Mexico, the high side of the mountain, gives smugglers a panoramic view of the border, the local police, the Santa Cruz County Sheriff's Department, and us, the U.S. Border Patrol.

The Border Patrol is part of the U.S. Immigration Service. Many illegals call us, *"La Migra,"* a truncation of the

Spanish word for immigration service (*El Servicio De Inmigracion*). At the Academy, I was conscious of being female everyday. On the border I am just another green uniform with equal opportunity to receive docile compliance from the average illegal, or a deadly bullet from a thoroughly pissed-off smuggler.

Every day upwards of fifty thousand people legally cross the U.S./Mexican border through a major port of entry. Another thousand or so illegally cross it by scaling the border wall, walking underground through drainage and sewage pipes, and stowing away on buses, trains, the trailers of semis, the hulls of boats, and occasionally in the empty belly of a diesel tanker.

Since most illegal crossings escape visual detection by human eye, cameras and motion detectors are positioned in strategic areas. The detectors are distanced back from the border because Border Patrol Agents cannot enter Mexico while on duty. The Mexican government would consider it armed invasion. The Mexican *Federales* would arrest us, and then the Border Patrol would fire us.

Like many American towns on the two-thousand-mile border with Mexico, Nogales is an official port of entry and is notorious as a thruway where kilos of drugs and hundreds of people are smuggled into the United States each day.

Mexican Joe is a smuggler. He hangs out between the two cities called Nogales. I don't know which one he calls home.

Traveling out of Nogales, the border wall changes, becoming fence, rope, and stakes in the ground, then nothing on the mountains and in canyons where I like to patrol. Out there the rugged enduring beauty of the terrain awakens the retro genes in me; they compelled me to plant flowers around my Ventura apartment even though the facility used a landscaping service. When I shared this with Marty, who is half Yaqui Indian, she said, "Out there you're one with eternity."

I agreed with Marty, but added more. "And I'm away from people."

"That's goes without saying," Marty quipped.

The first six months after leaving the Academy I patrolled the border one-on-one with a journeyman agent. Even though the logical part of me understood the necessity of this arrangement, the part of me that had cared for myself since I was five years old resented the eyes-over-my-shoulder approach. Another unsettling practice was changing work shifts before my body adjusted to the previous one. A new shift every four weeks, a new journeyman every two. On my second rotation, I was paired with Mr. Guzman; a Vietnam veteran turned federal agent.

"Would you report it if you accidentally crossed the border?" Mr. Guzman asked one day as we stood atop a ridge overlooking the port of entry into Mexico.

The harassment given me at the Academy had stopped, yet I knew some of the men to be chauvinist, bigots, and worse. Not having Mr. Guzman figured out, I didn't know if his was a trick question or idle curiosity. This uncertainty influenced my response.

"Right after you report yourself for calling illegals 'wets.' "

"Don't take that shit personally," he said. "You're good ole U.S.A. born and bred just like me."

True. But Mr. Guzman didn't look like a *nativo*. Put my tawny skin, coarse dark brown hair, and eyes the color of weak *guañabana* tea, in a room full of illegals from practically anywhere below the equator and I would look right at home.

CAROLYN WILKERSON

★ ★ ★ ★ ★

After Christmas and Three Kings Day, an innate nomadic urge awakens in the belly of peoples born to forage, and the northern exodus starts. By early spring there's virtually an unbroken queue of humanity paralleling the Trans American Highway and its connecting tributaries from Tierra del Fuego to the U.S. border.

In April, uncontrolled rainforest fires in Mexico and Central America spewed industrial strength fumes northward. By the fifth of May, smoke stalled over Southern Arizona and rained haze over a populace addicted to the sun. Two weeks without a daily dose of sunrays precipitated a change in residents similar to the northern neuroses occurring during winter months when days are short, sunlight is scarce, and behavior becomes unpredictable.

Still it was spring. Indigenous people had been migrating north since 300 B.C. when Hohokam Indians developed irrigation systems to grow crops in the area straddling the U.S./Mexico border and people settled here to farm. Today it would take more than a sky full of secondhand smoke to stop them from coming.

On May twenty-third, the skies were darker than ever. Then it rained.

Obeying the immutable laws of physics, rainwater scrambled down mountainsides and over roadways. Rushing to find its level, runoff rainwater left deep scars in its wake and formed ponds in old gaping scars.

Water ponds can be four inches or four feet deep and the difference is not always perceptible from the vehicle. We go around them when we can. Sometimes in slim canyons and arroyos, the only way is through.

The night of the big rain, Mr. Guzman and I worked eleven to seven. We were cutting signs, or tracking along

HASTA MAÑANA

Tricky Wash. The evening rain's gift was a clear night sky. Black-bellied whistling ducks roosted in cottonwood trees and there was a champagne chill to the air. Although we knew men, women, and children trekked northward, their journeying went undetected.

I had already put in a day's work, driving around looking for Mexican Joe. Now during the mesmerizing quietness of evening, I soon daydreamed of a long soak in a hot tub with a good book and an iced tea. Then a sensor triggered west toward San Antonio Canyon, snatching me out of my reverie.

Mr. Guzman and I responded.

He took the high trail over the ridge. I headed low through the canyon on a trail ideal for a hiker or a horse, but my '93 Ford Bronco jumped up and down over it like popcorn over a high flame. I splashed through a pond I couldn't avoid, then dropped into a rut, hit my head on the hard plastic corner of the sun visor, yelled, "Damn it. Shit."

A quick glance in the rearview mirror revealed only mussed hair. Probing fingers came back bloodless. I looked back to the road and saw horse tracks in the soft, wet soil. I quickly rolled down the window, stuck out my head and heard the animal snorting like he was running hard, carrying a heavy load. A drug smuggler probably heard the Bronco. Knowing the horse would go home, he smacked him on the rump to make him flee. Then the smuggler escaped over rocks, leaving no trace of his travel route. Even if I did find him, without drugs he had committed no crime and his only punishment would be a free ride back to the border.

But I could still get the horse, which if not stopped, would return to his stable across the border, drugs intact, and be ready to cross again *mañana* or the day after. I radioed my location to Mr. Guzman.

"Stay put," he said. "I'm on my way."

Mr. Guzman was being an alarmist, I thought. I wanted to be proactive. "The horse is in sight," I said. "He'll get away if I don't stop him."

"He won't get away. I'll be there in three minutes. I promise."

I couldn't remember the last time someone kept a promise they'd made to me but I did remember the three hundred or so pounds strapped to the horse would have a street value of about a quarter of a million dollars if it were dope. If it were pure cocaine it could kill a few thousand people. One snort had exploded Shaun's heart. The bottom line was this: the border was close and the horse would cross it before Mr. Guzman could reach me.

Not willing to risk losing the drugs, I followed the horse into a canyon just wide enough for my vehicle. I came out of an S-curve and the horse was illuminated in my headlights less than fifty feet away, snorting and prancing near the base of a cliff. I had to get closer, though, to block the opening to the canyon. A road pond was between us, but the watermarks were only eight or ten inches up the horse's legs.

Yes, I did consider the horse could have walked the shallow edge of the pond but only after my vehicle entered the water, sighed, and hunkered down. When it finally touched bottom, water was even with the hood.

"Damn it," I yelled and hit the steering wheel with my hand. I put the Bronco in reverse, and pressed the accelerator. Tires spun. Water churned. I switched to forward gear, accelerated, spun tires again. "Damn. Damn. Damn."

"Quiet," Mr. Guzman ordered through the radio. "Sound amplifies in these canyons. Everybody for miles can hear you whining like a girl."

Everybody translated into other agents who knew my dilemma and were laughing at me. I had to clear the pond myself. The door creaked when I opened it.

"Stay in the truck," Mr. Guzman barked. His tone sounded so much like Marty the hair on the back on my neck bristled.

The hubs had to be manually changed from two- to four-wheel drive, advertising the truck's age. I jumped out and waded to the front wheels, reached down and when I did, water covered all but my head. I changed to four-wheel drive, cursed the Service for not giving us newer vehicles, got back in the Bronco, put the transmission in first gear, and got enough torque to clear the pond.

When Mr. Guzman arrived, I was standing below the cliff next to the horse, his reins in my hand and a smug smile on my face.

Mr. Guzman stopped. He exited his vehicle one movement at a time, hands extended from his gun, eyes going left of me then up, left of me then up.

The third time, Mr. Guzman's eyes went left and up, my eyes followed his eyes and saw what he saw. I was on Mexican soil.

My smile vanished. My pulse soared like smoke in an updraft.

I looked back and up over my head, then had the sudden, pressing urge to void. On the ridge above us stood two armed men. They could kill us and no one would ever know who had done it.

Mr. Guzman knew our predicament before getting out of his vehicle, but instead of backing out and saving himself, he came forward, refusing to leave me there alone. *You will never be alone.* He did it to keep a promise.

Clearly illuminated by starlight, one man, swarthy and muscular, wore the dark fatigues of the Mexican Police. He aimed an M-16 straight at me.

The other man was tall and lean, his blond hair curled from the heat, and a five-inch scar connected his cheek to his chin. He swaggered even as he stood still. My blood iced. He fit the description Billy Rose had given me. *Mexican Joe.*

I couldn't think, I couldn't move. Marty didn't have much time left. She would die at peace, she said, if the man who had killed her grandson preceded her into hell. My plan had been to find Mexican Joe and kill him for her. For Shaun. For me. Since coming here, I had searched for him, driving Shaun's red truck until I felt one with the wheel. But to find Mexican Joe like this, to have him hold me captive, to have him kill me . . . Marty would curse me with her dying breath.

"Let the horse go," Mr. Guzman said. "Drop the reins. Now."

I came out of the daze and did as he said.

The horse did not move.

"Hit him," Mr. Guzman demanded. "Hit the damn horse."

I walloped the horse. He ran away.

"*La Migra,*" Mexican Joe laughed. "You whine like a girl."

Then I knew Mr. Guzman had tried to warn me about Mexican scouts hearing my vehicle, not agents. Mexican Joe had monitored our transmission with his sophisticated equipment. My stubborn need to prove a point would cause our deaths.

"Nice red truck," Mexican Joe said. "You drive like a crazy woman."

HASTA MAÑANA

My red truck? This was worse. He'd seen me when I hadn't seen him.

"*Hasta mañana,*" Mexican Joe said, then did an about-face and walked away.

The Mexican policeman backed away with slow, measured steps. When the tip of his gun disappeared from the horizon, Mr. Guzman spoke.

"Can you effing believe that?" He sounded incredulous. "They let us go!"

"*Hasta mañana,*" I whispered. Until tomorrow. You get to live at least that long. Then I will kill you for what you did to my Shaun.

Mr. Guzman looked at me. "You got a death wish or something?"

"I just meant there will be another time," I said. "Next time I'll be ready."

"For what? If you do see him again, your fire power will be no match for his."

Did Mr. Guzman know my insides churned like a butter paddle when I looked up and saw the gun aimed at me? Did he know all my training left me, my plan didn't matter, and I was reduced to a baby who just wanted to pee? If he didn't know then, he would know now if I recalled the bravado I'd broadcast to the winds.

"I'll get ready," I said. "If I have to buy my own gun."

Mr. Guzman wasn't fooled.

"Miriam," he said, using my first name against the rules. "Even men get scared. Some days, it's only with the grace of God we go unharmed. On those days," he said, "tough men are scared little boys who want to piss their pants."

He blotted the tears sliding down my cheek with his sleeve.

"It's smoke from the forest fires irritating my eyes, Sir. I never cry."

Mr. Guzman looked up at the clear sparkling sky, then back at me. "Sure." He changed focus. "Not that anyone would believe it, but don't ever repeat what happened here tonight. And don't ever disobey my direct orders again."

"Yes, Sir." I faked a smile, extended a peace offering. "The first shot of tequila at Elvira's is on me."

"The first shot is free," he said. "You buy the *chile rellenos*."

Elvira's Restaurant was at the end of Avenida Obregon, west of the border. Off duty agents frequented it, along with a horde of locals, tourists, and illegals.

It was a good place to look for Mexican Joe.

CHAPTER THREE

Once back in the Bronco, my thoughts raced all over the place. Even though I sucked up my humiliation in the face of Mr. Guzman, the voice of my own conscience would not be quieted. I had seen Mexican Joe with my own two eyes and I had done nothing. *Nada.*

Well yes, I had done *something*. I had come away from the encounter alive. I had lived to have another chance. And while he may have seen my red truck driving around Nogales, Mexican Joe did not know I was looking for him, nor did he know why. Then I thought, being an excellent tracker, I could find signs of Mexican Joe and the policeman. I could go look for them now.

The two men probably accessed the ridge from a point on the far side of the cliff where it was nothing more than a footpath offering little resistance except a steady uphill trudge. Maybe I could climb the ridge to where they had stood. Maybe I could track them to where they went. Maybe I could still get Mexican Joe.

Maybe. Maybe. Maybe.

But maybe never offered much hope to me, so probably not.

I sighed. The odds of me finding the exact spot where they stood on the ridge, after having driven eight or ten miles around the base, and have it be on American soil were astronomical. The chances of me climbing straight to this high, steep site were slim and none.

I cursed myself for blowing my chance to get Mexican

Joe, then drove the Bronco toward town. Though it had been less than two years, I felt like I had been preparing forever for a showdown with Mexican Joe. Billy Rose had cautioned me against it. Marty had told me it was a waste of time. Her solution: "If you want to get close to a drug dealer, buy drugs."

But Mexican Joe was not a dealer. Kids at school dealt drugs. Mexican Joe was a businessman. To stop him I had to have a business plan.

If I told my story to someone like Mr. Guzman and asked his opinion, he would say, "You can't stop the flow of drugs by stopping one smuggler. This Mexican Joe may be a businessman, but he's the middleman. Someone will thank you for removing him so they can take his place."

That's what Mr. Guzman would say if I told him my plan. He'd probably add, "What you're planning to do is at least as bad as what Mexican Joe does."

Well, I knew that. I'm not morally void. But knowing wouldn't stop me.

I turned the heat in the Bronco up a few degrees. The night air and my wet clothes chilled me to the bone. Or was I shivering because deep in my heart I knew this was not about removing a drug dealer from business so other children Shaun's age wouldn't buy them. This was about revenge as old as biblical lore. An eye for an eye. Mexican Joe's life for my son's life.

A year or so before his death, I began to think of Shaun as my son. I had grown up enough myself to experience true maternal longing and needs. Mr. Rose, Father Angelo, and I were going to tell Shaun I was his mother on his sixteenth birthday. I had steeled my nerves for his anger; I had prepared my heart for his rejection. My nerves and heart were just not prepared for Shaun's death the night before the big day. Even now pain rips me like a dull, rusted saw.

I grabbed the Thermos under my seat and took a hearty swallow of the boiled cornmeal drink of my youth. Then I sped the Bronco up an arroyo to the top of a hill, stopped, and got out. The Catholic indoctrination Father Angelo etched on my youthful brain gave me no comfort when pain was this great. In times like this, the spirits of my Indian ancestors chased me to open spaces where they communed with me in private. When I was receptive, they surrounded me, suffused me, and lifted me up above the frailties of my human body, as I let them do now.

Standing firmly on Mother Earth, I opened my arms wide and reached to Father Sky. With eyes closed, I chanted the mantra of bereaved souls and soon the essence of life eternal flowed through me, a continuum of past, present, and future. At once I was as dead as I would ever be, yet as alive as I had ever been.

For one serene moment the elements of earth, wind, and the passion of fire commingled within me as a universal oneness with no beginning and no end. I did not resent myself for failing in my mission. I did not grieve Shaun's passing. I did not hate Mexican Joe.

CHAPTER FOUR

The night I first saw Mexican Joe was to be the longest night of my Border Patrol career, "long" being a term defined as hard to endure.

After my ten-minute hilltop respite, I went back on patrol thankful Mr. Guzman was not going to report my infractions, yet at a loss to understand why he was lenient with me. He had never given me reason to believe I was one of his favored people, let alone someone for whom he'd risk his life or badge. How could I be? He'd known me less than two weeks, so why had he come into the canyon with death standing over our heads? Him, who preached, "Don't get into a situation you can't see a way out of." While none of it made sense to me, I didn't complain about him bending rules, when not bending them could mean my gun and shield. I couldn't give them up. They added legitimacy to my mission.

About three in the morning, the runoff of water subsided and the activity level stepped up. Visual detections of illegal crossings were so numerous no agent was free to respond to a sensor near the egress of one of the drainage tunnels starting in Mexico and ending in the Santa Cruz River on the U.S. side.

At one point I pursued a group of five illegals running down Grand Avenue, near the Mexican consulate. I rounded a curve on two wheels to see a manhole cover pop up in the middle of the street, five yards in front of the Bronco's front bumper. Jerking the wheel to the left, I missed the manhole but ran up on the curb and hit a eucalyptus tree, tires squealing to a stop. The boy who pushed up the manhole cover climbed out. He saw me in time to discern what I was and escape before I got to him. But he didn't. He had a fatalistic air about him, an eerie disorientation making him resemble a zombie. He was caked with whatever was in the sewer he had just exited, and smelled like it, too. Silent tears rolled down his grime-smeared cheeks.

"Is anybody else in there?" I asked.

"No importa." It's not important, he whispered. His voice broke. *"Estan muertos."* They are all dead.

Certain he was trying to get me to move on so his friends would not be captured, I waited ten seconds, thirty, then one full minute before realizing no one else was coming out of the hole. They must have heard our voices and hid in the sewer. I handcuffed the boy to the Bronco, radioed Mr. Guzman, and flashed the high beam of the flashlight down the manhole. Nothing. I lay down on the street and stuck my head into the manhole for a closer look. Nothing but fast-moving water.

When Mr. Guzman arrived, I had determined a name, Miguel; a country, Honduras; a status, illegal; and had heard a story that was making me sick to my stomach.

Miguel said the farmers back home set fires in the spring to prepare the land for planting. But the past year *El Niño* kept the rains away and everything was dry. So this year when they burned the fields, the fires got away from them and into rain forests containing a hundred years' worth of dead foliage, tree trunks, and grasses. Soon thousands of fires burned and there was no water to put them out.

Despite his obvious youth, Miguel was among the first to realize the more the fires burned, the fewer the crops; the fewer the crops, the less income for families who were already living on an average of five dollars a week. He knew it was time to go north. He said they successfully outwitted banditos, *federales,* wild dogs, and coyotes, and made it to Nogales, Sonora before the drenching rain. The group was afraid of the dark, smelly drainpipe, but the scout they had paid to lead them to Tucson had said it was "okay."

"Look how big it is," he had said. "They drive trucks into these things to dump garbage." Miguel had even seen tire marks at the beginning of the drainage pipe and a warm yellow glow deep in the darkness. But Miguel and his group could not know water rushing down the mountains earlier would end up in those same pipes. They were caught by surprise halfway through their underground journey, when millions of gallons of water exited myriad culverts under the town and entered the drainage pipe with them. The water forced mud and rocks and garbage and silt through the smaller section of the pipe like ground meat forced through a sausage press.

Miguel got lucky. Water lifted him up off his feet, high enough to catch the ladder rung near the top of the manhole; it carried the others away. "So much water," he cried. "They must to die."

Mr. Guzman's face relaxed. I sighed. Standing on the street you could hear water rushing beneath the pavement. *So much water.* Was it enough water to carry them through the drainage pipe to the Santa Cruz River? The city of Nogales is not more than a square mile; it would only take a minute or so for a torrent of water to enter and exit the drain. They could hold their breaths that long. Even if they didn't, they would be underwater so short a time the chance of them drowning was slim.

Mr. Guzman radioed an alert. Agents and emergency vehicles rushed to where the pipe emptied into the Santa Cruz River. The illegals would be angry at having to return to Honduras, but at least they would be alive to make the trip again. A third of them never made it their first try anyway.

I called transport to take Miguel to the facility to be processed for return to Honduras. Then I drove to where the drain emptied into the river. When I got there, everyone was leaving.

"As expected," an agent said. "They got away."

I jumped back into the Bronco and drove the streets of Nogales looking for signs of Miguel in every face I saw and soon realized I saw signs of Miguel in many faces I saw, but none had "illegal" stamped on their foreheads. Without it in border towns, it's near impossible to tell them from citizens. And sometimes it is impossible to tell Mexicans from Hondurans from Colombians, and so on. So I looked for taxis with people crammed to the ceiling, people with muddy shoes or skittish movements, or people who refused to look back at me. And all the while I couldn't shake the feeling of dread consuming me, couldn't extinguish the bile burning my gut each time I remembered the look on Miguel's face when he said, *"Estan muertos."*

Miguel believed his companions were dead. After looking in his eyes, his heart, and his soul as he said those words, I believed him. The others in Miguel's party were not walking the streets of Nogales. They were dead or soon would be if I didn't find them.

When I first arrived in Nogales, I wanted to know every foot of the border, every drainpipe leading from country to country, every hole in the wall, every gate in the fence where Mexican Joe could walk across, jump over, or crawl through. So I purchased street maps, aerial maps, forestry maps, mining maps, topical maps, new maps just off Rand

McNally's press, and old maps of the territory dating back to the first permanent Spanish settlement in 1752. I had maps of what the area looked like in 1821 when Mexico won its independence and the Arizona land passed from Spanish to Mexican rule, in 1853 when Mexico ceded the land to the U.S., and in 1912 when Arizona became the last of the contiguous forty-eight states. I also had a map of the underground sewer system for the city of Nogales, and that's the one I pulled out of the milk crate filing box I always carried in whatever vehicle I drove.

Studying the map, the logistics weren't hard to decipher. If Miguel's party crossed the border where he said, they wouldn't have been where I discovered him. Not ordinarily. Not with a seasoned scout. But this had turned out to be an extraordinary crossing and I did not know how many times the scout had made the trip. Men south of the border are as macho as those north of it and quite naturally think they can find their way to anyplace without consulting a map. When the economy gets bad enough, every man becomes a scout if the occasion presents itself. And each one promises a safe crossing. And most nights that could be accomplished. But nature owns riparian rights to the land. When water comes, water rules. It flows around what it can, and over, through, or in what it cannot. If someone unfamiliar with the sewer system was leading Miguel's group when water took the right of way, he could have gone in the wrong direction when he reached the juncture where all the pipes came together in the center of town and then led them to disaster.

If the scout led the party of illegals toward the noise of street traffic downtown, which he probably did, the pipes would have branched out in many directions and gotten smaller in size before reaching the river. So small, in fact, they'd have to travel single file, hunched over, then crawl. In the end they would barely squeeze through the opening lying down and it would be only with the force of water pushing them that they could get through at all. Tracing the major flow of water with my finger, I came up with three possible outlets and raced to check them. The second one was as full of mud, silt, and debris as the first, but the second one had the sole of a Nike clearly exposed. Even before pushing it with my boot, I knew it was still attached to a foot.

I screamed into the radio for help, then I threw it and my flashlight aside, fell to my knees and started digging with both hands. When my fingers clasped a leg, I recoiled from the cold, clammy latex feeling and threw up, but didn't stop digging until two sets of strong hands dragged me away.

By the time Mr. Guzman arrived at the scene with Miguel to identify the bodies, all nine members of the party had been unearthed by the street department crew. It took three agents to restrain the anguish battling Miguel's soul when the last body bag was unzipped for his identification. He set upon himself, scratched his eyes until they bled, and pulled his hair out in clumps when he saw Sonya, his equally young bride, who was three months pregnant with their first child. Suddenly Miguel's nationality and resident status were *"No importo."* It didn't matter. It's against policy to turn away medically needy illegals already on U.S. soil.

Miguel was sedated and taken to the hospital. He would be given medical asylum for as long it took his mind to return to him. Having no such escape from the reality before me, I returned to the station, where I remained hours past the end of my shift completing official forms. At three p.m., after having been on duty sixteen straight hours, I left for home. Since repeatedly declining the opportunity to be off, I was expected back in eight hours, ready to work my regular eleven p.m. to seven a.m. shift.

Heading north on I-19, the afternoon sun beckoned me to play. Although there was nothing inside me with enough enthusiasm to respond, I did pop in a Ramsey Lewis CD and drive around with my windows open to settle my nerves.

I remember thinking, the employment bulletin Billy Rose gave me read: A Federal Law Enforcement career offers challenges, variety, and excitement . . . The Border Patrol is the first line of defense in preventing illegal entry into this country.

The bulletin didn't state how badly people want to enter the U.S., nor did it list the hardships they endure or sacrifices they make to do it.

I'm sure illegals anticipate getting caught, being returned to their country, and maybe being caught again before finally achieving the goal of making it across the border.

I don't believe any of them ever expect to die breathing sand.

For the first time I entertained the idea that completing my own mission might require an extreme personal sacrifice from me, too. As acceptance settled deep in my soul, a little rational part of me asked if I really believed my mission was on par with Miguel's. Was it worth giving up my life?

It was a question I would not let myself consider.

CHAPTER FIVE

I arrived back at the apartment complex, parked in my assigned space, and carried my gear upstairs. The mud on my boots had dried; still I pulled them off and left them on the catwalk outside the front door. I had another pair to wear back to work—I looked at my watch—in six hours. Stepping inside the foyer, I stopped on the entry tile to remove gun, shield, and belt, and placed them on the floor; then I stripped down to my underwear, putting the soiled uniform in a basket kept by the door. I picked up the standard issue items and took them into the bedroom, placed the ammunition magazine in a drawer, the shield on the dresser, checked the chamber of the gun, then put it in a safe and turned the tumbler several times.

"Why do you do all that?" Marty once asked. "There're no children here."

There were no children. Shaun had been the only one I'd had. I was the only one she'd had. "Suicide is high in stressful jobs, and stress and guns don't mix," I told her. "If I have to go to too much trouble to kill myself, I won't do it."

"You're too ornery to kill yourself," Marty snorted.

"I hope you're right," I said. I didn't say to Marty I was more worried about her than me. With the right combination of stimulants and the wrong frame of mind, she might do anything. She didn't appear to have suicidal tendencies now that she was in constant pain, but I was taking no chances.

I ran a tub of bath water, added enough Clorox to disinfect but not harm me, washed my face with a Noxzema medicated pad, and then slathered it with vitamin E oil. I put on a vintage Clapton disc, lit some candles for Miguel's baby and placed them around the tub, eased myself in, and then immediately fell asleep. An hour later I had slid so far down in the tub, water slurped up my nose when I breathed, nearly gagging me. I flailed around the slippery tub until my hand got purchase, and pulled myself to an upright position. I got out, hocked up bath water from my lungs, and then sopped the blue tiled floor with my robe until it was dry.

I wrapped my head in one towel, my body in another, changed Clapton to Pieces of a Dream, and stuck the bowl of oatmeal Billy Rose had made for me that morning in the microwave. The hot cereal bubbled. The aroma was enticing, but I ate without tasting the maple or the brown sugar.

I lay on the couch and slept three hours more before awakening to my own screams.

I had dreamed I was buried alive.

CHAPTER SIX

"Miriam." My neighbor, Mrs. Kim, was knocking on the door and yelling. "You okay? You okay?"

Clutching the blanket around me, then dragging it on the floor and tripping on the fringe, I stumbled to the door and opened it. "I'm okay. I had a bad dream."

"Not surprised," she said. "Saw TV news." She shook her head. "Velly bad."

Originally from Korea, Mrs. Kim owned the Circle K convenience store down the street. Her husband taught at the University of Arizona in Tucson. They were both here legally; however, I had my doubts about some of the multitudes I saw going in and out of their apartment.

She ushered me back to the couch like a mother hen nudging her chicks, said, "Rest," and pushed me toward the couch. The pillow still held the shape and warmth of my head. "Bling you tea."

There was no point telling her not to, she would do it anyway.

I dropped to the couch, put my head into my hands and cringed at the image that popped into focus. The horror in the drainage pipes reeled through my mind like a "velly bad" movie, to quote Mrs. Kim. I didn't know at the time but it would be weeks before the image dimmed and then only because a new horror eclipsed it.

I did know why so many chanced crossing the border, however. I heard it every day. *"Un trabajo,"* they said. A job. And, there was always someone willing to pay illegals under the table to work below minimum wage. I had discovered that, unlike Americans who think they are entitled to something for nothing, illegals would do anything to help their families. Even die.

According to Marty, my father had an important job requiring him to make many sacrifices, one of them being me. Wherever he is now, I have his tall, slender build and his eyes. Sometimes when I close them I try to see what he is looking at, what he has seen. When I was young I tried to see Marty and me from his perspective. Tried to answer the question, "Leave them or take them with me?"

When I was six, Marty had said, "He didn't leave you. He left me." Which of course made no sense to me. Then when I was ten, the explanation was clarified. While tipsy, Marty said my father never even knew she was pregnant. He discovered her smoking a pipe not a part of an Indian ritual ceremony and ran away from her as fast as he could, unknowingly leaving me in her womb getting high right along with her. Marty said she would get away from herself, too, if she could. Yaqui Indians are indigenous to Sonora Mexico and southern Arizona. Marty has never been further than Tucson.

After that day I never again blamed my father for abandoning me and when, as a teenager, I stepped from the mire that was sucking me under, I fantasized about him, making him fearless and determined and smart, traits Marty did not have. My fantasy father imbued me with all the good stuff Marty couldn't give me. Admittedly, it sounds childish, but I was still very much a child and with reality a filament loosely spun around me like a spider's web, I needed something, even a fantasy, to hang on to.

I survived being born to an alcoholic mother and was a healthy toddler. Then when I was five, Marty started giving me overdoses of Dimetapp. "Just to make you sleep," she whispered her sad apology in my ear. "Marty's stepping out for a while."

Marty promoted me to beer when I was eight, and when it no longer knocked me out, she let me toke a joint. My complicity in all this was taking each one from her just as eagerly as I did her breast when I was a baby. But thank God I don't have an addictive personality. In the end, it may have saved my life.

After having dreamed I was buried alive and waking up screaming, my head felt like it always did the morning after Marty gave me too much beer and I had to get up and go to school. And I always went to school. School was a solid reality consisting of smells, sounds, textures, feelings, and 3-D visuals offering tangible verification of normalcy.

Of course the school buildings and teachers changed when Marty moved us. But wherever I was, the edifice called school was a beacon offering refuge to a soul desperately seeking rules and routines, nourishment, and adults who were dependable from day to day. Perhaps that's why I became a teacher. Perhaps that's why the regime at the Border Patrol Academy inspired rather than restricted me.

Marty was born an American citizen. She grew up internalizing The Great Society entitlement attitude and when she couldn't find a man to take care of us, she took handouts from the state. She was reported to social services several times for child neglect, but she always convinced her caseworker she was on the verge of, in the midst of, or just emerging from a breakthrough in her recovery. "I need her," she would plead. "My baby is all I have. If you take her away, there's no reason to get myself together."

Marty would throw in a tear or two and the caseworker would let me stay. After all, she never beat me, going to school every day kept me fed, and the school nurse kept me healthy. Maybe Marty messed up from time to time, the worker probably reasoned, but the child looked well nourished and didn't have bruises and marks and therefore couldn't possibly be neglected any more than the rest of "them." Again I was compliant. Marty had told me enough bad things about foster homes to prompt me to agree with everything she said when the caseworker talked to me. But after I had Shaun, Father Angelo insisted I go to a foster home he selected for me in San Diego. "Otherwise," he said, "I will talk to social services myself." Father Angelo didn't make idle threats; he got things done.

Now, I hear some people with my beginning say; "It's not my fault. I was a crack baby. I had a deadbeat dad and a mother who was not much better. So get off my case. I got a right to be fucked up."

Yet, I've seen others with my beginning go on to do great things, as though their environment, or their parents, or their situation buoyed them up instead of weighing them down. When I got away from Marty and drugs, I looked to those positive role models for inspiration. But deep down in my heart, I now know I made what I made of myself so my son would not be ashamed of me like I had been ashamed of my own mother when I was growing up.

I'm not hesitant to admit to being ashamed of Marty because as deep as feelings of embarrassment ran, parallel to them ran other equally deep feelings, and one cried out for her love and approval. Since being on this mission, I seem to have everything I need from Marty. The thing is, if I accomplish my mission I will have done much worse than she ever did, for she never hurt a soul more than she did herself. Sometimes I wonder if prospects of me doing something more despicable than she prompts Marty to show her love for me, now.

Not being a psychiatrist, I can only conclude that the motives for Marty's behavior are still mummy wrapped around her own soul, hiding her own demons. Even without knowing all of them, I have forgiven her for what she did to me. And I hope someone will someday forgive me for what I plan to do to Mexican Joe.

The only thing I like about my past is the music. When other memories roll over me like the tide over sand, they deplete my emotional reservoir and the residual effect drains me. Billy Rose usually intercedes between me and memories with half-baked jokes and backrubs, but he wasn't here when I woke up screaming. Truth is, he's not home more and more, or maybe it was always this way and I never noticed.

Billy Rose is a computer genius. He is a freelance programmer and has a home office, but with laptop, cell phone, and pager, he can and does work from anywhere. When I finished the Academy, he had already leased a furnished apartment for us in Green Valley. I'm not ungrateful, mind you, but given a choice, I would have selected an end unit away from the pool and playground. Sometimes the children's squeals and squabbles drift up to my ears and into my heart and I long for a time with Shaun that I never knew.

And when I hear a child yell, "Mom," my gut clenches. Not once in his lifetime did Shaun ever call me Mom. I was, "Val. My brother Billy's friend."

I rose from the couch, went to the kitchen sink, and splashed cold water on my face. Sometimes I feel weak and helpless; yet other times I think I'm a stronger person than either Marty or my father. I'm not a slave to love like she was, nor do I run from love like he did. I just don't have love, not romantic love anyway. I just have Billy Rose.

Like a magician's apparition, Miguel's face appeared to me. His primal screams, his heartbreaking sobs resounded in my ears. The blood from his self-flagellation seemed to redden my hands. Poor boy. In one night he lost all reason to live. And now, just like me, he clings to memories that bring him pain.

Miguel and I had something else in common. Both of us were consumed by the grief of our loss. Unfortunately for Miguel, he was just beginning the grieving process. I was far enough along to want to get revenge.

I didn't think Miguel was to blame for the deaths of his wife and child. Yet, I sensed he took the burden squarely on his shoulders. He suffered guilt as surely as if his hand had poured the sand which suffocated them. Miguel could not escape the blame suffusing his being as completely and as destructively as a flood raging through an ill-constructed house.

My job with the Border Patrol gave me the means, resources, and training to find Mexican Joe and make him pay for Shaun's death. Is that what Miguel's mental breakdown was doing for him, making him pay for the deaths of his wife and child?

My head throbbed like it was being banged with a rubber mallet. Miguel wasn't a murderer. Mexican Joe was a murderer. He was cold, detached, unfeeling. Miguel was a young man impassioned by love; a man committed to his family.

Mexican Joe was scum.

Miguel was a young man any woman could clasp to her bosom, love with all her heart.

Again his face appeared before me, and for an instant I felt as nauseous as I had the instant I unearthed the first cold leg from the soil. Before I gave in to the urge to vomit, the doorbell rang. Mrs. Kim called out, "Miriam."

I gulped whatever wanted to rise. "It's open, Mrs. Kim."

She came in carrying a tray covered with a napkin and broadcasting aromas bespeaking of Korean delicacies. "Hot tea. Food. You eat."

"Mrs. Kim, you didn't have to do this."

"Had to," she smiled. "Billy arrange before he go Mexico City. He doll."

"Yes," I said, suddenly feeling betrayed. "He's *quite* the doll." A regular Chatty Cathy who didn't tell me he was going to Mexico City.

Then I had to smile for reacting like a neglected wife. Billy Rose and I lived together for convenience and had not been lovers for a very long time. He was free to come and go as he pleased.

I shooed Mrs. Kim away, ate, dressed, and went to work early.

CHAPTER SEVEN

When Mr. Guzman and I left the station at eleven-thirty p.m. the air was crisp, the sky was clear. My body was just beginning to adjust to working during my normal sleeping hours; in a little more than two weeks the shifts would change again.

Mr. Guzman hadn't been a bad journeyman. Still, I didn't have a fix on his personal views about anything. All our conversations had been about, concerning, or involving the Border Patrol. That's why his actions that night surprised me.

Halfway through the shift we had detected no illegal crossings. It wasn't only us, either. No one all day had apprehended illegals going north, an occurrence as rare as a blue moon. Spring up, fall down was the little ditty we sang. Of course many illegals crossed twice a day, commuting to work. I remember my first day in the field. My journeyman and I apprehended a family of seven, processed them, and had them transported back to the border. That night I stopped in the Burger King in downtown Nogales and there sat all seven enjoying Whoppers and fries.

Tonight was my first experience with inactivity and it was disconcerting. But people south of the border are largely Catholic and deeply family oriented, so it wasn't hard for my overactive imagination to envision thousands of them approaching the border to illegally cross, then upon hearing of the tragedy, stopping where they were to mourn the deaths.

HASTA MAÑANA

Just thinking about the bodies, arms, and legs compacted in the earth as though prepared for fossilization, eyes and mouths stuffed with sand, and pockets full of sewer waste, caused my eyes to sting.

I quickly changed focus so the tears swelling my heart would not overflow my face. I would not, could not succumb to weakness two nights in a row. Thinking of Mexican Joe always made me angry. I thought of him. Wondered why he was called "Mexican Joe." Perhaps Mr. Guzman had heard, perhaps he knew. "Do some of the drug dealers have street names?" I asked.

He looked at me like I was dumber than tumbleweed. "They all do, Miss Valencia. What's your question?"

Realizing my *faux pas,* I gulped and tried to fix it without admitting it had happened. "Can't put anything over on you, can I?" I lightly laughed.

"Not when you ask stupid questions," he replied.

I tried to think of a way to phrase my "real question" without revealing my true question.

He tired of waiting and walked to the edge of the plateau on which we stood, lifted the night goggles hanging around his neck to his eyes, and slowly turned three hundred and sixty degrees. A mild breeze danced across the tops of the trees below us. An updraft mingled with his cologne and brought it back to me. Somewhere a coyote threw his voice, ventriloquist style, across the desert floor. A pygmy owl asked, "Whooo," then all was silent once more.

Mr. Guzman returned to his Bronco and leaned against it. The vehicle was parked parallel to mine, about four feet away. I leaned against the driver's side of my vehicle, he leaned against the passenger side of his, putting us about three feet apart.

Thirty-six inches is a long way if that's how far your canteen is and your leg is caught in a crevice, rendering you immobile. Thirty-six inches is far if an international borderline divides the distance and what you want is on the other side. But thirty-six inches isn't far if you're feeling vulnerable, like I was, and there is a six-foot-two, big *chili* kind of a guy with feet planted wide and arms casually crossed around his muscular torso, standing in front of you.

Every female intuition I had told me Mr. Guzman was going to make a move on me. Of course, it would end up being his word against mine, if I decided to object. If I didn't, no harm no foul.

While he did nothing, my anxiety level escalated. Then I realized he *was* doing something. He was staring me down. Good old-fashioned body language intimidation. She who blinks first loses. She who looks away first loses. She who breathes first loses.

After the third loss, I cleared my throat and decided to take the heat off me the only way I knew, by asking an unrelated question.

"You've been around Nogales for a while," I said, lazily drawing a stick figure in the sand with the toe of my boot. "Have you ever heard of a drug smuggler named Mexican Joe?"

He didn't alter his stance. "And if I have?"

His tone was sufficiently antagonistic to annoy, putting me on equal footing with him again. Even good-looking men can't charm me when I'm ticked off.

"If you have," I demanded, "then tell me what you know about him."

He said, "If you want trouble, he can give it to you."

That wasn't what I wanted to know, but if Mr. Guzman knew that much, did he also know it was Mexican Joe who had held us captive the night before? If he did, why didn't he say so now? More importantly, if he knew, why did he come into the boxed-in canyon with Mexican Joe standing on the cliff holding a gun?

My thoughts bombarded my brain and fragmented, but I took time to sort them out and only verbalize what I meant to say this time. "Do you know Mexican Joe when you see him?"

He unfolded his arms. "Don't you think it's time you stopped playing games, Miss Valencia, and tell me what this is about? If you don't trust me, why bring it up?"

Sighing heavily, I gave him the stripped down, friend-of-a-friend version.

"Stay out of it," he warned. "You're supposed to patrol the border, not dispense vigilante justice."

Vigilante justice. My heart hurdled up into my throat. I breathed long and deep to maintain my composure. "Does vigilante justice apply if it's closer than a mere acquaintance?"

He leaned forward from the waist, cutting the thirty-six inches in half. The source of the cologne the wind had brought back to me earlier was his smooth shaven cheek, now clearly positioned within the perimeters of my lifespace comfort zone. His breath burst warm on my nose when he said, "If that's your reasoning, Miss Valencia, you need to decide here and now if you want to live or die."

"You're just like a man." I said, which was the most uncharacteristic thing for me to say. "I should have known you wouldn't understand maternal instincts."

He stepped back, looked at me for a long time; questions ran through his eyes, the twitch of his nose, the lick of his lips, but none were verbalized. Instead he asked, "What does your boyfriend, 'The Roseman,' say about this?"

I had never mentioned Billy Rose to Mr. Guzman, or to

any of the agents. How and what did he know about him? Instead of asking, I said, "Billy Rose is not my boyfriend."

Suddenly I was sorry I said as much as I did.

Though he may have had a million questions and even more suppositions floating around his head, Mr. Guzman didn't have any incriminating evidence pertaining to my plan that could get me fired. If he did blab, it was my word against his.

I needed to be alone. My eyes searched the distance and soon found my favorite place. Apparently Mr. Guzman knew this, too. He immediately said, "I saw you up there last night. What were you doing with your arms stretched up to the sky?"

"Meditating," I said, hoping that would be all he wanted to know.

"Med-i-ta-ting," he elongated the word and smiled. "And what do you get out of that?"

If he didn't know, I didn't have the time or the inclination to reform a skeptic, and that's what I had read into his voice. "Only what I put into it," I said.

"You're not trippin' on peyote-inspired visions when you meditate, are you?"

"I'm not a Navajo mystic," I said. "I'm part Yaqui."

He reached over and touched my forehead. "What else is in there?"

I stepped sideways, increasing the distance between us.

He smiled. He knew he had won again, and until then I hadn't realized the "game" had restarted.

The spot where his finger touched my forehead pulsated and I, without rhyme or reason, remembered no man had touched me since Billy Rose.

It had been a long time since Billy Rose.

Far away, the coyote again threw his voice into the night.

HASTA MAÑANA

I felt the loneliness in his song. The sky sparkled with celestial diamonds casting a soft candlelight glow. There was enough of a chill in the air to make me hug myself for warmth. All in all no time to tell myself the man in front of me is sending out his own desperate wail as lonely as the coyote's song.

The pygmy owl asked, "Whoooo?"

I breathed in slow and deep. I assured myself the man in front of me would not be the one to end my dry spell, and although my intent had been to smirk, I must have smiled.

Mr. Guzman raised an eyebrow. "Is something funny?"

"No."

"Did I ask an improper question? I mean I don't want to be accused of harassment or anything."

"It wasn't improper."

"Embarrassing?"

"No."

He leaned forward again. His nose was near my cheek. If I turned my face to the left, his lips would touch my lips.

"Then why the hell don't you answer me?" His breath tickled my nose.

I sneezed in his face.

He jumped back.

I looked at him defiantly. "If I answer, will you let it go?"

"For now."

I looked down at my boot. "My mother is half Mexican, half Yaqui Indian. My father is half black, half Cherokee."

"Oh," was all he said.

And for some reason I was offended. "What's that supposed to mean?"

"It means you're mystic, salsa, and soul." He smiled. "A combination that could be very hot and very dangerous."

So great was my irritation, body hair itched in places I wouldn't dare scratch. If fumes came out of my ears and evolved into smoke signals, it would not have been a surprise.

We were standing high on a hill, miles from everywhere, close to nothing; yet, when Mr. Guzman took a step toward me, I started to feel crowded. Threatened in a way I'd felt once in a bar, and a few times at the Academy when male trainees tried to corner me coming out of the shower at three in the morning.

My hand instinctively went to my gun and caressed the butt.

I stood my ground. "As long as you don't cast any voodoo spells on me," I said with bravado, "you don't have to worry about me burning anything of yours."

He took another step, with a long stride this time, and passed me close enough to knock me off the mountain with one swift bump of his hip. But he chose to glide past, not even ruffling the air between us. He looked through his goggles out over the terrain, turned three hundred sixty degrees, looked all ways, saw nothing, and didn't seem surprised.

"The people will come," he said, talking about illegal traffic. "The news of the deaths traveled far and fast. As soon as they think no one's looking at the border, activity will surge like fans rushing to meet the winning team after a soccer game."

He turned and looked at me. "Do you know anything about surfing, Miss Valencia?"

This question from left field caught me off guard. "Why would I know anything about surfing?"

He smiled. His even white teeth gleamed like pearls. "You're a California girl, aren't you?"

"Yes," I mumbled. "You just got me confused."

Then I was embarrassed. Although my thoughts *were* confusing, I hadn't meant to tell him. I had had plenty of men make passes at me before but never as smooth as he did, and never leaving me as disconcerted as I was. In the end, I felt he had spurned me before I had a chance to spurn him.

My usual ability to correctly assess a situation had failed, unsettling me. I much preferred being one step ahead of the men in my world. It gave me a sense of security and preparedness, thus arming me with avoidance strategies if needed.

This man sight, as I called it, had taken me successfully through the Academy. True, the males there were fresh out of high school, fresh out college, fresh into life and as easy to read as a pre-primer. Mr. Guzman had been in the Border Patrol for two years and had worked eight years as a police officer in Dade County, Florida before that. The scuttlebutt had him leaving Miami one day before a cache of drugs turned up missing from the evidence room.

When I first heard the rumor, I had tabled it alongside the one labeling me a dyke because I never dated any of the agents. Why I suddenly remembered the rumor about him was just as mysterious to me as how Mr. Guzman knew about Billy Rose.

Down below a twig snapped, an animal scurried through the underbrush. Hushed whispers wafted up.

"They're moving," Mr. Guzman announced and pointed down below where, through the goggles, everything looked green and white, but perfectly clear.

A figure darted across a ravine, then another and another.

Mr. Guzman's arm arched to the left about forty-five degrees. "That's where they will cross the border," he said. "That's where they will end up," he added. "Let's go. You can be the welcome wagon lady."

Jumping into our separate vehicles, we rolled down the cliff, engines off. At the bottom he went toward the border crossing point, I went to the other spot he had indicated. When the radio pulsed against my body, I put the earphones in my ears, hit the button and Mr. Guzman said, "Lights."

I turned on the high beam spotlight and lit up a human wagon train heading north. Mr. Guzman was caboose, I was engineer, and thirty-nine illegals were between us, blind as bats from the light and reaching for the sky.

Transport came and took the illegals to the station where they were fingerprinted, photographed, and the paperwork necessary to return them to the border was completed.

For a while I forgot about what almost didn't happen atop the plateau.

CHAPTER EIGHT

During the after-work drive, I replayed the psychosexual drama atop the plateau, and then I reluctantly deduced my overactive imagination had been on the loose again. I asked myself the following questions: Did I read more into what happened than what actually happened? Did he say or do anything blatant? Was it a case of my subconscious putting thoughts into my head? And, I shuddered to ask; did wishful thinking fill in the blanks?

Mentally dissecting the whole of my encounters with Mr. Guzman, I came up with not a word or even a tone out of line; not an accidental brush against my body, not a question with a double meaning, *Nada*. And, even before tonight, he had never before given me any reason to believe he had more than a perfunctory professional interest in me. An interest so superficial that maybe, just maybe, he could, if he worked hard at it, maintain sufficient interest to continue the two-week period he was to be my journeyman, and the whole non-incident was conjured up by my mind. Ergo, I was the one to feel the loneliness in the coyote's yodel, not him.

Only about a hundred of the seven thousand Border Patrol Agents are women. Rumor had it that Mr. Guzman reduced the last one in his charge to a blubbering mass of protoplasm before her two weeks were over.

Well, he couldn't do that to me. Perhaps knowing this, he decided to use another male domination trick. Seduction.

I had stopped at a signal light and the thought of Mr. Guzman trying to seduce a non-romantic like me made me laugh out loud right there in the truck. The people in the next car over looked at me like I was crazy. And maybe I was a little bit mad, but mostly what stirred in me was intrigue. I wondered just how far it would have gone, with the requisite full moon and starlight winking "romance" and the slight wind in the trees whispering "cuddle."

When I got home, I would ask Billy Rose what he thought. That is, if he was back from wherever he had gone. Speaking of intrigue, Billy Rose's mysterious side was showing again. Once again confirming his basic character had not changed much since I met him. But mine had, and the more I changed inside, the more things outside of me looked different. For example, Billy Rose and I were no longer involved, but we did live in the same space. Since my maternal side kicked in, I had started needing to know where he was, and if he was all right. But explaining it to Billy Rose in a way that did not elevate his personal expectations from me would take a miracle of biblical proportions.

Right now I wasn't aligned with people who could walk on water.

CHAPTER NINE

Between the ages of seven and ten, Marty and I lived with her boyfriend Conrad Elliot in a prosperous suburb of Tucson. Marty called him, "Colonel Connie," and he was stationed at Davis-Monthan Air Force Base. We lived far enough away so his co-workers did not drop in unannounced, but close enough for Conrad to commute to work and to the officers' club, where he spent a substantial part of his weekend. He was, after all, a married man playing the part of missing his family while he was away from home.

"Uncle Connie," as I was instructed to call him, was a pleasant enough man who couldn't keep his hands off Marty's tits and ass. He was the one who told her, "Give beer to the kid to make her sleep."

Marty had learned the rules of engagement of female survival at an early age and was eager to please her man, or whoever's man she was with at the time. She pleased Conrad until he purred like a well-sated tomcat and he rewarded her with mock animal fur, costume jewelry, and promises of forever just as fake.

Marty tried to teach her survival skills to me. Her expectation? I would end up being some older man's play-pretty just like her. I rebelled from the beginning.

"You've got to want what your man wants," she explained when I asked her why she wanted him to put his hands on her "private parts."

Since my eight-year-old mind couldn't fathom wanting him to do that, I asked, "What if I don't like it?"

"You just got to pretend you like it," she said. "Men don't know the difference as long as it makes them feel good."

"What if it doesn't make me feel good?"

"As long as the bills are paid," she said. "It doesn't much matter how you feel."

That's when I discovered the hair on the back of my neck could prickle like the bristle on Conrad's boar hairbrush. Something as personal as how you feel should matter. At least that's what I read in the teen magazines on the shelf of the drugstore in the mall.

By then, I had watched Marty gush and giggle when Conrad squeezed her for over a year. I had observed with growing frequency the number of times she cooed and waited on him when he fretted and whined. It was then I guess I subconsciously decided I was not a doll to be manipulated by a grown man. At any rate, whenever it was learned, it was cast in stone before I met Billy Rose, and it would come between us in later years.

The summer I was nine, the Rose family moved next door to Marty, Conrad Elliot, Marty's dog Cuddles, and me.

Billy Rose was taller and two years older than I, but I was the scrappier of the two, even then. He was as pale as a ghost; a scrawny squirt with long blond hair that curled on the end and bounced when he jumped after the kids yelled, "Boo."

Mr. Rose was stationed at Fort Huachuca Military Base. A die-hard enlisted man, he said he declined base housing "to live among regular people." He wanted his family to "experience the local culture, otherwise what's the use of moving from place to place."

After a month or so, Marty had her own opinion. She

said, "He doesn't want 'Sam' knowing he beats the shit outta his wife and kid."

In those days Marty used what some people now call "recreational drugs." Looking back from the perspective of an adult who's been around the block a few times, it's uncanny how often Marty's insights were as keen as any intellect I've ever known, and she only had a GED.

Mrs. Rose was not crazy about the local culture, the city of Tucson, or, seemingly, Mr. Rose. I think she learned the same survival games as Marty, but her execution was different. At any rate, she rarely came outside without big dark glasses, long sleeves, and enough pancake make-up, Marty said, "to cook waffles."

More importantly, Mrs. Rose never seemed to notice her husband ogled other women, including Marty, or him "accidentally" touching me from time to time, or her child soaking up the local culture faster than a paper towel sopping up a bad spill.

Billy Rose was the nurturer of our duo, the one to teach me how to match clothes so they looked good together, and the one to buy the sanitary napkins when the monthlies ran red. The one to nurse me the few times I did get sick. Over the years we experienced sorrows and joys linking our lives and our souls much deeper and more permanently than the mere fact that we made a child together.

When Conrad Elliot came home one day and announced he was being transferred to Seattle and not taking us with him, Billy Rose was as upset as Marty, but for a different reason. What it meant to him was I had to move back to Colonia and away from him. We went to different schools then, but Billy Rose rode his bicycle to my house every afternoon. If it rained, he took the bus.

Billy Rose followed me into the lost world of drugs when I foolishly thought being like my mother would make her love me like a mother. At least, that is my hindsight on the years eleven through thirteen. But I have to admire Billy Rose. He sat at the feast of degradation but he did not eat the food. I've never to this day seen him snort or shoot a drug or toke a joint. When I became pregnant, he made me understand what drugs could do to the baby, then held my violently shaking body while my system exorcised itself of the deadly chemicals.

Billy Rose and I have a symbiotic relationship and at different times he has been my father, mother, sister, brother, lover, Jiminy Cricket, guardian angel, and best friend. I would give him my kidney, my money; my life if he asked, but the only thing he has asked for is my heart. I can't give him my heart because the intuitive part of me knows Billy Rose is flawed. Like a pet that has been abused, he is good most of the time, but sometimes he isn't. The only reason I'm safe from his impulses is because he loves me.

A deep thinker, Billy Rose could play a complete game of chess in his mind and never forget a move. He would have made a great general except that the combat boot of his father kicked the fighting spirit out of him when he was young. I was his protector, earning his undying devotion the first day of school when I beat the snot out of Joey, the playground bully who insisted upon calling him "Rosy" as in girl.

Billy Rose could calm me down faster than a Valium. He could set me off as predictably as an alarm.

I should have known, reporting the events with Mr. Guzman atop the plateau would enrage Billy Rose. But I had no way of knowing it would anger him beyond the worst outburst I had ever seen, and that had been when Marty accused him of killing her dog, Cuddles.

CHAPTER TEN

Today when I reached the second floor landing to our apartment, it was ten o'clock in the morning. The day was sunny and clear, but the blinds were closed, as they had been at ten o'clock the night before. When he was home, night or day, Billy Rose opened every blind and window in the apartment as though he had to prove he had nothing to hide. Sometimes you literally could see everything because he walked around buck naked, his personals swinging in the wind, little coconuts swinging on a substantial tree trunk, giving the women on the far side of the pool a treat.

The elation I'd experienced in the truck had now deflated. I opened the door to the apartment and a slash of light sneaked across the carpet and climbed the opposite wall. It reversed its course when the door again closed, leaving me standing in light as subdued as my mood. The aura of the apartment was cold and stark, and didn't seem to welcome me home. Noticeably absent was Billy Rose's reggae music and the mouth-watering aromas of his home cooking.

Not thrilled about being alone and also having to cook, but aching for a long soak in the tub and a cup of hot chamomile tea, I started to undress.

The quick and sudden intake of a breath that wasn't mine alerted me to danger. While my right hand removed my gun from its holster, my left hand hit the light switch, and I swiveled forty-five degrees to face the bedroom.

There on the bed sat a naked Billy Rose, computer on his lap.

Despite a loaded and cocked gun being pointed at him, he did not speak or move. He maintained his silent stance so long—past the time necessary to make his point of trusting me—I knew something was wrong. Or, at least not right.

In absence of an explanation, my conscious looked to the only wrong thing it knew: what I had been thinking about on the drive home. The moment that thought surfaced, the secret knowledge registered in my eyes, eyes locked with Billy Rose's eyes. It was as though I couldn't stop the flow of knowledge from leaping from my mind to his mind until I was sure he knew every thought I had had, putting Billy Rose on the plateau with Mr. Guzman and me, and in the truck with me when I secretly admitted to enjoying the flirtation as hungrily as a dieter relishes the smell of pastries still baking in the oven. My soul was bare to Billy Rose and he now knew the nightmare of his nightmares had finally come true. Just for a second my heart had achieved synchronicity with a heart other than his.

At least, this is what I imagined in the ten or so seconds without words. Having experienced feelings of guilt as though I had betrayed him, I quite naturally thought he knew me so well he would automatically know. Truth is, Billy Rose may just as well have been scared shitless. A 40-caliber semiautomatic Beretta pointed at your head can do that to you.

I broke the silence, which obviously oppressed me more than it did Billy Rose with, "What the hell are you doing here?"

"I live here," he said. "What the hell are you doing, robbing me or arresting me?"

I lowered the gun, removed the bullets, and tried to laugh. "Neither. It's dark in here and I wasn't expecting you. Besides, nothing's cooking in the kitchen."

The last reason was supposed to be a joke, a tension breaker, but Billy Rose didn't see it that way. He closed the laptop, set it aside, and stood up, never once losing eye contact. "I'm not your personal chef, Miriam." He walked from the room toward the kitchen.

"You're right." What else could I say? "I'll call for Chinese."

He picked up a small, gaily-wrapped box from the kitchen counter. "You know carry-out stuff has monosodium glutamate in it."

I knew no such thing but if it got him into the kitchen, I wouldn't quibble.

"Here." He extended the box to me. "I brought you something from Brazil."

The box was red and shiny and wrapped with silver and gold ribbons. A tiny silver filigreed bell dangled from a golden bow. He knew I collected bells and I knew he bought only the finest silver. But something in my mind clicked and up popped a scene from childhood when Conrad Elliot stayed away all weekend without calling. Marty was livid when he returned Monday night. He let her rant and rave and throw things not intended to hit him.

He pulled out a pair of golden hoop earrings and said, "Here. I brought you something." And this time they were real gold.

Marty took the earrings and, as far as Conrad was concerned, that was the end of it. Peace offering tendered and accepted. Case closed.

Marty understood this male/female guilt eradication protocol. She accepted the gift without further comment.

Now my hand wanted to reach out and take the box, my ears wanted to hear the tinny ping of the bell clap, my eyes wanted to feast upon what was so precious it could be even more special than the expensive, unwrapped bell. But a red flag saying, "Don't be your mother's daughter," waved.

I couldn't take the box.

Billy Rose seemed to understand my hesitancy and said, "Miriam, I'm sorry for not telling you I was going to Sao Paulo." The cloud covering his face, hiding the Billy Rose I knew, lifted and he came back to me. "I just got back," he smiled, "and was billing my clients when you came home.

"You finish what you started," he continued. "I'll cook. After breakfast you take a long soak and I'll give you my special massage."

Special massage. More capitulations, then the rite of contrition is completed. I wasn't having it. "We need to talk," I said, reining in my urge to take the box.

"We'll talk later," he said. "First you relax and eat."

"Now," I demanded, "and cover yourself up. I'm going to open the blinds and you don't need to make all the women looking up from the pool horny."

He smiled but put on a gray Chinese silk robe.

See, Marty, I thought. When you don't know the rules, you can make up your own.

CHAPTER ELEVEN

Billy Rose didn't roll over and play dead for me, but maybe he thought he had more to lose than me so he acquiesced first. The truth is I was the one with everything to lose. My friendship imposed a tremendous burden on his small shoulders, but he held them straight. He could easily have found someone else to boss him around like I did, but for the role he played in my life, he was irreplaceable.

Billy Rose was not perfect, however. He'd get territorial sometimes. And sometimes he'd whine and complain about the load he carried for me so I would express compassion. Admittedly, I owed him, but my heart did not collateralize the debt.

"That boy acts like he owns you," Marty once said when I was pregnant. "He's sneaky, too."

"What's that supposed to mean?" I asked.

"I know men," she said. "There's more to William Joseph than meets the eye." She always called Billy Rose by his given name.

"If there is," I wistfully said, "I sure wish he'd show it to me."

"No, you don't," she replied. "He's more like his father than you know. It just comes out different."

Mr. Rose was an insecure bully who controlled his family with verbal and psychological abuse, interspersed with occasional punches and smacks to reiterate his authority. "I can't see Billy Rose acting anything like him," I said.

"Well, Miriam, you wouldn't," Marty said. "You're just a child. But when you've known as many men as me, you learn to understand them. William Joseph manipulates people by setting the stage, like one of those movie directors, so things turn out his way."

"He's just a boy," I protested. How could he do the things Marty suggested? He couldn't be this person she was describing and I not know it, could he?

All Marty would say was, "He's a devious boy. I just hope that baby you're carrying doesn't end up like him. Anglos say the apple doesn't fall far from the tree."

I prayed the Anglos were wrong. Even though Billy Rose claimed paternity for my child, he was not the biological father. But I hadn't told Marty.

After donning his gray Chinese silk robe this morning, Billy Rose sat on the couch with me and we talked about things that had begun to annoy me. Specifically, not knowing where he was or when he would return. I put it in the context of housemates and home security. "Just look what almost happened this morning. I could have shot you, thinking you were a burglar."

He agreed to post his itinerary on the refrigerator alongside my work schedule. Nevertheless, it did not escape my detection that he had told Mrs. Kim he was going to Mexico City and he just told me he'd returned from Sao Paulo. Which city did he visit? Did he go to both? It was surely a possibility. He billed his clients for his travel expenses and frequently bought first class tickets at the last minute.

Then Marty's words, "He's a devious boy," came back to me. Maybe he didn't go to either. So even though he posted his itinerary, it didn't guarantee where he'd be. I de-

HASTA MAÑANA

cided that, in the vast scheme of things, his location was of no consequence. If I got hurt or killed, he could answer his page from anywhere in the world. Anyway, this morning was about me feeling guilty for what my conscience had earlier told me was an indiscretion. But to tell the truth, the further I got from the actual event, the more the feeling of guilt dissipated. Nothing really happened, except for a few moments, I felt something I had never before felt. I had wanted to relive the moment with Billy Rose, just like I had shared the sensation of my first period, my first kiss, childbirth, and all the other firsts in my life. Maybe I should have had a female best friend. Maybe then my life wouldn't have gotten so complicated.

Taking the gift from Billy Rose would tell him I had diffused any lingering feelings I had, and we were okay. I took the red box. Inside was a beautiful pin I at first thought was an Egyptian scarab. But Billy Rose explained it was a real dehydrated beetle whose wings had hardened into a shell and had been lacquered over to keep the body intact. Then it was mounted on a backing to make a pin. The peacock pearl colors shimmered blue-green-black-pink-orange with a luminescence indicating they were the natural colors, not a clay kiln-created patina of glazed porcelain. The pin had been made in Argentina and was quite expensive.

"It's unique," I said, and it was. "But you shouldn't have." And he shouldn't.

"My client gave me a bonus," he boasted. "I can afford a few thousand for a trinket."

A trinket, maybe, yes. A dead bug? No way. Not for me. I can't even look at the butterfly display in the museum without cringing. There was no way I was going to wear a dead beetle on my lapel. I put it back in the box. "The azure blue in the mix of colors reminds me of the way the night sky sometimes looks," I said, and segued into my story about the previous night without further comment on the pin.

If I had been paying attention, I would have seen the dark brooding cloud return to Billy Rose's sky blue eyes. Then I would have been prepared when he asked, "Why're you telling this to me? So I'll make you quit?"

"You're always saying I'm so cold and unresponsive," I said. "I just thought you'd be happy to know I really can feel like a woman.

"Besides, you didn't make me take this job," I added tersely. "And you can't make me quit. You can't make me do anything."

"Right," he said. "But I can make him sorry he ever touched anything of mine."

The vein on Billy Rose's temple pumped hard and fast. The white of his eyes had a reddish hue and his teeth were clenched in dogged determination.

I reminded him, "I don't belong to you, Billy Rose."

He jumped up, knocking KoKopelli, the Kachina doll, off the coffee table. "And you won't belong to him," he said. "He's a common thief hiding behind a badge." Now the veins on his neck seemed to bulge as large as his small neck, and spittle flew from his mouth as he spat the words at me.

The intensity of Billy Rose's anger startled me, reminded me of his father in ways I had never before experienced.

"Mr. Guzman is my journeyman," I said. "I'd never date my supervisor. Besides, he was trying to intimidate me, not put another notch on his bedpost. Anyway, I don't have time for that kind of a relationship."

"Don't I know it?" He continued to look at me as though he could see into the tomorrows of my mind to a time when

HASTA MAÑANA

I would be ready and leave him behind. There was no such information inside me for him to find; after a while he gave up, calmed down, and was sane again.

See, Marty's voice said in my head. *I told you the family is crazy.*

Marty had diagnosed the Roses when Cuddles died. She and Conrad had planned to go away overnight. I had to look after the dog and wouldn't be able to go with Billy Rose and his family to Saguaro National Monument to see the giant cacti and look for roadrunners. The day before all of this was supposed to have happened Cuddles' body was discovered near the mauve rock garden in the side yard.

Mr. Rose said, "Maybe the mutt got hit by a car."

But there was no blood and Marty insisted, "He doesn't chase cars. One of you maniacs did it." Then she screamed, "A Rose by another name is a Nut."

Marty was too distraught to go away for the weekend. She said she needed to be alone and sent Conrad to the officers' club and me with the Roses. She was convinced that Cuddles had been strangled to death and said, "I know that boy killed my dog."

"But why would he do it?" I asked. "He loved Cuddles."

"He wanted you to go with him more than he loved Cuddles," she said. "He knew I wouldn't go anywhere if my dog was dead."

"If you know he killed the dog," Conrad said, "call the police."

"Nobody's going to believe what I feel in my heart and can't prove," she sniffed.

"Then stop giving that boy a bad name," Conrad said.

Marty stopped giving him a bad name, but she never stopped believing he did bad things.

CHAPTER TWELVE

An hour later, when Billy Rose opened the apartment door to leave, heat blasted in like air from an opened pizza oven. Welcome to summer, I thought, southwestern style. The air is so hot and dry it can cause a nosebleed, my personal life's shot to hell, and I'm as harried as a roadrunner chasing a gecko.

I closed the door behind Billy Rose, went to the window, and watched him drive out of the parking lot. All in all, the morning had been a disaster. First Billy Rose scared the shit out of me and I responded by drawing down on him. Then he lied about where he had been and gave me an expensive gift made out of a dead bug. Then I lied about how exquisite the gift was, as if I would wear it anywhere but to my grave. To make matters worse, I tried to talk to him about really personal stuff that both scared and delighted me and we ended up fighting like an old married couple with unresolved issues simmering on the back burner.

Sure, we'd had spats before, but this one was different. This time it was though invisible lines had been drawn in the sand and neither of us had known about them until a sensor went off when the lines were crossed. Then the lines sank beneath the sand, and search as we did, we could not find and re-cross them.

Yes, we smiled and hugged and swore we were fine, but the grumbling in my gut didn't feel like we were. When Billy Rose suddenly decided to go to Mrs. Kim's Circle K to buy coffee, my intuition said it was more to get away from the echo of my disclosure than it was to buy French Roast. I assured him the tiff was over and done with, but as soon as Billy Rose drove out of the parking lot, I went to his computer, intent upon snooping. If he were billing a client, like he said, and didn't clear the document folder on the desktop, the information should still be there. It didn't take a computer genius to know that much. If it was still there, I might be able to discover where he'd been.

Though I wasn't tracking Billy Rose's movements per se, a premonitory flash motivated me to know more about where he went and what he did. Maybe knowing would help me understand why he told Mrs. Kim one story and me another. Was there a woman involved? Was that why he was so secretive? It would be great if he were romantically involved with someone; then life would be easier all around when love finally came to me.

My fingers slid down the side of the laptop, pushed the button on the side, and the hard plastic top popped open. I turned on the computer, clicked on start, then scrolled the cursor to documents and clicked again. *U.S. Department Of Justice Personnel Office/Guzman, Enrique.*

Uneasiness rushed through me. What did Billy Rose want to know about Mr. Guzman? I remembered Billy Rose saying: "He's a common thief hiding behind a badge." What else had he learned?

I hadn't discussed the rumor about Mr. Guzman stealing drugs from the Miami Police Department evidence room with Billy Rose. I hadn't taken him to the station or introduced him to any of my co-workers. Where did he hear the rumor? Why was he snooping in Mr. Guzman's personnel file?

As questions zipped through my mind, the uneasiness settled in the pit of my stomach. Something was going on and I was out of the loop. Knowing Billy Rose, it could have been as simple as trying to find out everything there was to know about Mr. Guzman just because the man spent eight to ten hours a day with me. But that didn't explain how he got into the DOJ computer.

Noting the absence of an invoice file in the document folder, I went into the program folder to find the database where he kept a client list. But when it was clicked, the computer beeped and the screen went blank. The cursor appeared in the upper left corner, along with the phrase, "Enter Password."

That was the end of my snooping, which was good. Just then one of the women around the pool yelled, "Hey, Billy. Put some baby oil and iodine on my back."

He'd returned from Circle K. He would be upstairs in a few minutes.

I shut the computer down, closed the cover, and then ran to the bathroom, stripping as I went, turned on the shower, and got in despite the water being cold.

Billy Rose came into the bathroom several minutes later. The water was hot and the room was steamy by then. I was lathered, head to toe. He came right over to the tub and jerked back the curtain.

Jumping as though he scared me, I flung my waist length hair so it slopped sudsy water all over his freshly pressed chinos and matching tee. Served him right.

He glared at me. "Were you bothering my computer, Miriam?"

"A little privacy, please. How can I use your computer in the shower?"

"It was moved."

"Oh, that." Closing my eyes and sticking my face under the showerhead, the water hit full face. Water sloshed out of my mouth as I talked. "It was on my side of the bed," I nonchalantly said. "So, I moved it."

He reflected a few seconds. "Oh. Okay."

"What you said about Mr. Guzman before," I ventured. "How did you know he was accused of stealing?"

"Easy," he bragged. "I made files on all the people on your duty roster."

"Really?" The uneasiness gripped me again. "And how did you do that?"

He laughed. "When you know as much about computers as I do, you can find just about anything. For instance, if I have a name I can get an address, then a telephone number, then a Social Security number, DMV records, birth records, credit reports, taxes, and so on, and so on. The information highway exits onto my computer screen."

He started to leave, then turned back. "Would you like to know his wife's name?"

"Fuck you, Billy Rose."

"Anytime," he started to remove his shirt. "Now would be good."

I snatched the curtain shut.

"I thought not." He whistled softly and closed the door to the bathroom.

I rinsed my hair and stepped out of the shower just as the printer came to life. By the time I was dry, the front door closed. I walked into the kitchen for a glass of orange juice and saw a note taped to the refrigerator door next to my schedule: "I have gone to New York. Be back in two days. Take a four-day weekend and go with me to Bogota when I return. I miss us. BR."

Bogota was out of the question right now, but the intent was appreciated and I smiled. I missed us, too.

Mentally Billy Rose and I had been inseparable since we

met and we were probably still invincible against the world. It was just between us that the fabric of a united front was becoming threadbare. Then it occurred to me, the "us" I missed was the two children who had made their way through the maze of adolescence and survived, despite wrong turns and near misses we would reminisce about until senility set in and took the memories away. But the boy and girl who successfully navigated that sea of trial and error and made it safely to the shores of adulthood were different people than when they embarked on their journey.

At least I was different. Billy Rose was pretty much as juvenile as he had been then. As a child, I had been left to my own resources, causing me to act more grown-up than I really was. What made our duo dynamic, early on, was Billy Rose nurturing me and me protecting him. That relationship had suited both our needs then. But before Shaun died, the whole process of internalizing and embracing motherhood changed my attitudes faster than my behavior could adjust. It confused me and, though he never said, it must have confused Billy Rose as well. But this I did know. A grown-up woman needed a different complement in her life than a girl pretending to be a grown-up woman, as surely as she needed different clothes and hairstyle.

There was one thing wrong with this amazingly clear insight. It illuminated a conflict of conscience. I liked having Billy Rose pay the bills, do the laundry, cook, and basically pamper me like Marty should have when I was growing up.

But under the circumstances, was accepting his generosity the right thing for me to do?

The room closed in around me, suffocating me with old French Roast coffee smells, Obsession cologne, and computer paraphernalia in every conceivable crack and crevice. Even my clothes confined and restricted me. I needed air, room, and my own space, full of my things, smelling of me.

When I finished high school and went to Cal State, in Northridge, California, Billy Rose went too. When I got a job teaching kindergarten and moved to Ventura, Billy Rose went too. When I came to Green Valley after finishing the Academy, Billy Rose was waiting for me. We'd known each other for twenty years and had lived together for the past ten. Except for nineteen weeks at the Academy, I'd never been on my own.

Maybe it was time I learned to be as independent as I acted. For sure, I'd have to acquire a taste for domesticity or hire someone to clean up after me, which I could do even without the several hundred thousand dollars Billy Rose declared each year. At the very least, with Billy Rose in New York, then Bogota, I would be alone for about a week.

For seven days I could work on the puzzle that is my existence; step one in building a new foundation for life. And I could look for Mexican Joe, a chore Billy Rose never seemed to have time or interest in doing. Just two weeks before he'd said to me, "I'm sorry I ever told you about Mexican Joe."

"Then why did you tell me?"

"I thought you needed closure," he had said. "A person to blame for Shaun's death. I wanted you to get on with your life, Miriam, our life, the way it used to be."

He had added, "I never thought you'd stalk the man to inflict revenge, especially since what happened to him was Shaun's own stupid fault."

The bite in his words ripped my heart, drawing silent, hot tears, which drowned my words in my throat.

Billy Rose never noticed me wince.

"It was too late, anyway," he continued. "What you set out to do. You would've spent the rest of your life trying to make it up to Shaun and he still wouldn't have been the son you wanted, not one you would've been proud of.

"He was too much like his father for that."

CHAPTER THIRTEEN

I went to bed after Billy Rose left, but sleep was as elusive as the question rumbling around in my subconscious was vague. Then the question solidified, forcing me from the bed to the telephone.

I punched in a number. When the clerk in Personnel answered, I identified myself with both Social Security and badge numbers and asked, "Can personnel records be accessed on line?"

"It can be done," the clerk said, "but you can't do it yourself."

"Why not?"

"Well," she hesitated. I envisioned her fidgeting in her chair, maybe looking around for help. None forthcoming, she continued, "You'd have to know passwords and access codes and things like that. And before you ask, I don't know what they are and no one here who does know is going to tell."

Naturally.

But they may not have to tell.

"Is there a way around, a back door, maybe?"

"I doubt it." She sounded young and naive. "I mean with all the safeguards nowadays. This is the U.S. Government, you know."

"Humor me," I said. "Could a hacker get into the personnel files?"

"He'd have to be a fuckin' computer genius," she said and hung up.

He absolutely was.

CHAPTER FOURTEEN

At each change of shift, agents assemble at muster so the Patrol Agent in Charge can give updates and new information necessary to doing our jobs. When I reported for the eleven p.m. to seven a.m. shift, we were told illegal crossings had intensified. A tractor-trailer had been stopped at the border that morning with ninety-six people in the trailer. Illegals were jumping on trains and scaling the downtown wall and boldly running through the main port of entry, as though they knew a massive frontal onslaught could not be stopped. Sure, some would be sacrificed, but two or three out of every four might get across undetected.

We concluded, either they were compensating for time lost during the lull after the bodies were found in the storm drains, or many more people were realizing what Miguel realized early on and were migrating north. Whatever *El Niño* meant as a weather phenomenon, it meant devastation as an economic indicator, at least south of the border.

And as frustrating as the statistics were, we knew the main reason so many people came in the first place was because American employers were willing to pay them under the table. Just as many unscrupulous Americans were willing to sell illegal identification, enabling illegals to get legal employment at the prevailing wage. The simplicity of the problem was laughable; the complexity defied explanation. And as one still grappling with the moral issue of who really owned the land, I was not able to craft a solution.

Simple or complex, however, the problem was doubly

frustrating to me because I worked overtime most days, then I had to finish the paperwork, filling out Form 1-213 for each illegal apprehended. This documentation is needed to justify my job. I don't mind doing the work, but by the time it's finished, I'm too tired to look for Mexican Joe. And tired or not, overtime is not time-and-a-half or double-time pay. The remuneration is much less in the Patrol.

The other moral problem I'd begun to have probably stemmed from my indoctrination into the cult of kindergarten teachers. I was starting to view illegals as individuals with special problems and needs and not as criminals, per se. Hell, the government didn't even classify them as criminals. The most that happened to the average illegal was that he or she was fingerprinted, photographed, then sent back to the border of his or her country. Unless they smuggled, raped, stole, or killed, the same illegals could be apprehended over and over and over again, making the southern border a revolving door. Spring up, fall back. Cross illegally, get paid illegally, go home for the winter and relax.

When Mr. Guzman and I left the station, the solar oven had cooled and outside actually felt good. In Oaxaca and Chiapas more than fifty large forest fires still burned out of control, making the sky a little hazy, yet it was still clearer than Mr. Guzman was.

"Things are not what they seem," he said as we approached the vehicle garage.

"They usually aren't," I retorted. "What are you talking about?"

"You ask too many damn questions," he said. "That's both your answer and your problem." He sighed. "I've been looking around in NCIC's computers, searching for your smuggler," he continued. "If he's as bad as you think, the feds should have info on him."

Another fuckin' computer genius, was what I thought; what I said was, "And?"

"And you'd better watch your step. Look in the faces of real people for your smuggler," he said, "stop looking for people who don't exist."

He opened the door to his vehicle and got inside.

Out of his earshot I said, "Well, fuck you very much, Sir," opened the door of my vehicle, and got inside. Yet another male sovereign had laid down the law for me.

I drove off into the night to meet Elisia Marielle.

CHAPTER FIFTEEN

The desert has something for everyone.

If you are a philosopher, you can stand below its vastness and ponder the age-old question of which came first, the chicken or the egg, God or man. If you are a scientist, the mathematical precision of the universe and predictability of natural celestial occurrences can awe you.

And if you just love nature, a clear southwestern night sky can sate all of your esthetical cravings for color and form and design as the sky cocoons around you, a gigantic planetarium offering golden ripe shining baubles you want to pluck from the sky.

But the desert floor is a very different phenomenon. There the wind blows swirls of dust or hordes of grasshoppers; mesquite bushes and hedgehog cacti co-exist, boulders and cattle rest; and wild pigs, mule deer, or roused tarantulas dart here and there. When you are lying-in-wait for illegals to cross the border, images at ground level can become muted, distorting what is alive and what is human. Rolling tumbleweeds or organ pipe cacti can look eerily like people, and a huddled up person can look like a rock.

That is why night vision technology is indispensable.

Night vision goggles convert light into electrical charges and intensify them. These intensified charges are then converted back into visible light images, which appear green or orange or black. This electronically enhanced sight helps to distinguish illegals from the landscape; it also makes barbwire fences and *cholla* cacti and desert animals easier to discern. Take my word for it, running headlong into a barb, whether it's a wire fence or a five-ton cactus, means you can be punctured, sliced, or diced as effectively as if it had been done with a knife, blade, or ice pick.

Night patrol is safer with goggles, so I made sure I had them that night, which was to be my last night on the eleven p.m. to seven a.m. shift. It would also be the last night Mr. Guzman would be my journeyman, and his conduct and efficiency report on my performance was due the next day. The worst thing I had done under his supervision was go into the canyon after he told me not to, and then inadvertently step over the border.

Since Mr. Guzman had told me not to mention the incident and I hadn't, I had to believe he would not cite me for it now. After all, he would have to explain why he waited so long to report the incident. At least I hoped it was true.

He should at least consider my willingness to work overtime, as well as the fact that together we seized over six hundred pounds of marijuana and apprehended two hundred and thirty-nine illegals during the two-week period, and let them balance out my little indiscretion. I would never again do anything so stupid, I vowed, if things just worked out this time.

Little did I know, making such a vow was itself an act of stupidity. There is no way we can look into the future and say with absolute certainty what we will or will not do. At least I can't. Circumstances always seem to rule.

I'm not sure when things started to change for me, but the seeds of change must have been there inside, waiting for fertile ground to grow. I do know, however, whatever else happened the night I clawed the pads of my fingers raw, trying to dig those people out of their mud graves, the seeds germinated. Until then, revenge was all that mattered to me. After that night, executing my job responsibilities with extreme sensitivity became as great a need as my need to find Mexican Joe.

When Mr. Guzman and I left the vehicle garage, I turned left onto Mariposa Road, drove up to the signal light, turned right, rounded the I-19 curve with squealing tires, passed the Mexican Consulate, and crossed over to Grand Avenue. The storm drain there is big enough to drive into, but it rapidly diminishes in size as it goes under the city, then comes out again in Mexico. It is frequently used to cross under the border.

As I approached the gaping mouth of the concrete pipe, a man darted out of the darkness and ran straight into the side of my Bronco.

My heart pounded. I feared the worse. Before I could ask if he were injured, the man got up babbling, *"¡Venga conmigo!"* Then he grabbed my arm.

This is a first, I thought, *an illegal turning himself in.*

"¡Venga conmigo!" he repeated. Come with me.

I didn't go with him. That course of action could prove disastrous for me.

"¡Por favor, Oficial. Mi esposa esta enferma!" he said. Please, my wife is sick.

Was this a new kind of shell game, a deception? Divert the attention of *La Migra,* then a whole passel of illegals run out of hiding and into the U.S.?

I still didn't move. *"¿Donde esta ella?"* Where is she?

"¡Por favor. Ayudanos!" he begged. Please help us. *"Mi esposa se va a arrivar."*

He'd upped the stakes. Now his wife was having a baby in the storm drain. He would only pull this ruse on me. All men think there is some genetically encoded cellular disposition that turns all women into sap when the baby button is pushed. How, then, could one woman not help another woman having a baby?

Well, I could be as cold and hard as the men. There was no way I was going into a storm drain to be ambushed or to let a group of illegals pass without me seeing them. Or, God forbid, step into Mexico again, wearing a gun.

A cry as urgent and painful as a calf that's just snapped her foreleg in a cattle-crossing grid assaulted my heart. I didn't know if the woman was having a baby or not, but I did know she was hurting. I have never before been so scared of doing anything in my life, but the adrenaline flooding my veins pushed me to the mouth of the storm drain. It was pitch black in there and I couldn't see more than a few yards, and somewhere beyond that was the borderline, which I also couldn't see.

The woman screamed again, weaker now. Still it set my teeth on edge.

"*El bebe*," she cried. "*¡Lo viene!*"

She was having the baby.

"*Ayudanos*," the man begged, then grabbed at my arm.

I didn't move fast enough; he snagged my Maglite flashlight and ran into the storm drain.

Bringing the night goggles to my eyes I followed his image, outlined by my flashlight, into the tunnel until I saw her, about a hundred feet back, lying in a pool of blood that seemed to widen before my eyes. She had lost so much she would be unable to remain conscious much longer. The baby was already delivering too early, if she lapsed into unconsciousness, she would have no chance of surviving.

The man threw the flashlight to the ground, fell down beside the woman, and tried to cradle her against him. For the first time, I saw he had only one arm. At the point

HASTA MAÑANA

where they were in the tunnel, he had to stoop to stand. With only one arm, he would never be able to get her up and out by himself.

Without realizing it, I closed the distance between us.

"*Banditos,*" the man explained as I neared him. Robbers had attacked them about halfway through the storm drain, taking their money and extra clothes. When the robbers tried to take the shoes from his wife's feet, she fought back. They knocked her around, into the wall, and to the ground, snatched her shoes, and ran.

The man said they had been told the baby would need special care right after birth. Having no money or insurance, they decided to cross the border to work in the fields for the remaining eight weeks of her pregnancy. Then they were going back home. But now the baby couldn't wait. A few minutes after his wife was beaten, labor started.

The woman was about five-two and weighed about one-eighteen pounds. I could bench press more than that, but it never entered my mind when I scooped her up and carried her back to my vehicle. I propped her against the front wheel and radioed for help.

"*Vamanos.*" I told the man and pointed toward the storm drain for him to go. His wife would be taken to the hospital but he would be taken to the station to be processed then taken back to the border. The storm drain was a shorter trip.

The man hesitated. He wanted to know if his baby would be born in America.

"*Si,*" I told him. Your baby will be born on U.S. soil. She will be a citizen.

He kissed his wife and cried like a baby himself, then disappeared into the dark recess of the drain just as the ambulance arrived.

CAROLYN WILKERSON

If anyone ever suspected I created an instant citizen, they never said anything about it to me. Until now I have never told anyone, including Billy Rose. But what else could I have done? If I had left the woman in the storm drain, both she and the baby would have died, if not from childbirth then from infections contracted from the sewer water flowing through the drain. If they had gone back into Mexico, they wouldn't have been much better off than being left in the drain.

By the time my shift ended, the woman had given birth and the baby had been named Elisia Marielle. Both would be in the hospital a while, but should be fine.

When I heard the news I was elated. Then I remembered each middle-class American taxpayer already pays almost eight hundred dollars a year for the care and feeding of illegal aliens. I hoped they would forgive me for adding this little one to their tax burden.

Somehow I knew God already had.

CHAPTER SIXTEEN

The city of Tucson is flat and ringed by four distinct mountains. Once you learn the face each mountain wears in the different seasons, orientation is easy and you are never truly lost. But that is not why I love Tucson.

I was born in Tucson General Hospital, went to school in Tucson until I was thirteen, and met the best friend I have ever had in Tucson. But those are also not the reasons why I love the city.

I love Tucson because it has an eclecticism unduplicated anywhere else in the U.S. Archeologists say its earliest identifiable inhabitants came here from Asia thousands of years ago, via a land bridge now submerged beneath the Bering Strait. Those nomads neither claimed ownership of the land nor destroyed its character. But in 1839, Friar Marcos de Niz, an Italian priest, and his African manservant, Estevanico, claimed ownership of the area for Spain. Since then the inhabitants have set about trying to make the land conform to their demands as diligently as a tyrannical potter tries to force elegance into clay predestined for brick. Yet the patina of its character is so intrinsically imbued in the land that carving it out, digging it up, selling and stealing it, fighting on it, flying four flags over it, has not dulled its edge.

The city of Tucson is large enough to have a metropolitan flair, yet small enough that people have not become its main attraction. It is a valley of sand, sagebrush, and cacti. It is twenty-one different Indian tribes, blacks, whites, Mexicans, Hispanics, Asians, and every other ethnic group, thanks to the proximity of Davis-Monthan Air Force Base, the University of Arizona, and the various mining ventures, archeological digs, and retirement communities.

Within minutes I can be at the Tucson Mall or in the Santa Rita Mountains. When a summer day gets too hot, night falls dramatically, dragging the temperature down with it. Winter is cool but not frigid; spring is a feast of fragrance after the rains come and the valley is awash with flowers of yellow, white, green, and red.

The Anglo God must have loved this area because He sent the Mormons to harness the rivers to turn the arid desert lands into fertile farms. And Indian gods forced the mountains to rise so high into the sky the San Francisco Peaks can be seen from one hundred miles away. They, like the Navajo Mountains on the Utah border, are spiritual points, which enable the Navajos to relate to the universe, thus giving the mountains a much deeper meaning than their raw beauty.

In fact, the San Francisco Mountains are home to some of the Kachinas, the Hopi gods, represented by colorful dolls, which are sold everywhere in Tucson, including the gas station where I bought KoKopelli, whose flute Billy Rose broke when he knocked it from the coffee table yesterday.

Despite my love for Tucson, too many bad things happened to me there for me to ever again call it home. So when I moved back to Arizona after a sixteen-year absence, I made my home twenty miles south of Tucson, where the memories are not so personal. At least once a week, though, I take Marty to Tucson to the doctors, to Sam's Club, and to visit Father Angelo. It's a time for us to catch up, but sadly, looking at her and hearing her talk is a painful reminder of how her body and spirit are deteriorating. To cleanse my soul of the sorrow her illness visits upon me, I go to the Afro-Cuban Dance Studio and surrender to the will of the drums.

South of Tucson, the edge to Arizona's character becomes as jagged as the rocks on a new mountain range. Daylight savings time is not observed, road signs are in metric, and every other truck has a gun rack in the back, usually cradling a rifle. These cowboys and girls live for the range, the mines, and the pecan groves. They landscape with skull bones from cattle, garden with gray and beige sand, plant mauve colored rocks for flowers, and build houses of dirt. They make mountains with mine pilings and monuments of inhospitable plants.

All this information scrolled through my mind as I snuggled under the covers of our king-size bed and waited for the propitious moment to ease from restfully reclining to chores and duty without disturbing the serenity I had achieved. It was the first day of my weekend, though it was only Thursday to everyone else. Since I would start day shift when I returned to work, I would not go in until seven a.m. Sunday. Hot damn. Three days off.

When I arrived home at eight-thirty that morning, I had been bone tired, weary, emotionally sacked, and lonely. Here I was thirty years old, attractive, intelligent, competent, fluent in three languages, and credit worthy. But I had no home of my own, no children of my own, and no man of my own, three visible signs of personal failure, per Marty's rules. Then I had meditated, crawled into bed, and unceremoniously put Marty and her ideas about what makes a successful woman out of my mind and sank into the most heavenly sleep.

Once awake, my first thought was to get up and go get

Marty. I always took her grocery shopping on my first day off. We were not the greatest mom and daughter team because I couldn't pretend our past never happened any more than I could ignore what her future would soon bring. But all things considered we did okay.

Helping Marty to get Social Security disability was the most self-esteem-building thing I could have done for her. She knew she didn't do right by me early on, she said, and she would have felt like shit having to take handouts from me now. And she categorically refused to take money from Billy Rose, which should have fanned the fires of my curiosity. Marty had lived off the generosity of men all my life. Why exempt Billy Rose? He made more money than anyone she had ever known.

The only thing Marty ever truly wanted in life was to be a lady. So now she had her dignity; she had a home health aide, whom she called her maid, and she finally had a small but nice place of her own in Rio Rico. She didn't have her requisite man, but Marty said she'd had her share of men and with one foot in the grave, a man, now, would just put the other one in there faster. Of course, that tune later changed, but not in the way I would have expected.

The shrill of the telephone ripped my veil of serenity. But it wasn't Marty. It was the hospital in Tucson. I had given them my business card in reference to Miguel. He wanted to see me.

I agreed to go to the hospital early that evening to see him, never once considering what effect the visit might have on Marty.

CHAPTER SEVENTEEN

Today, I had to satisfy two masters, Marty and Miguel, so I let logistics prevail. It was easier to go down I-19 ten miles to Rio Rico and pick up Marty before going up I-19 twenty miles to see Miguel in Tucson General Hospital.

At least that was my thought as I planned the rest of the day. Later though, I couldn't help but wonder if forces more mysterious and less scientific were influencing the decision. Miguel had wanted company, the hospital social worker had said, and she knew of no one but me. But once he and Marty met, they reached around me to each other and he latched on to her like a newborn to his mother's breast. Considering they had nothing in common, they bonded on a level it takes most people months, maybe years, to achieve.

Marty, on the other hand, said they had everything in common. "We both need somebody to hang onto," she said.

"You've got me," I flippantly said, trying to keep my seared feelings close to my heart. I did everything I was supposed to do for her and more, and here she was talking about "needing somebody to hang onto" like I was no closer kin to her than one of those faces in the picture frames she bought at the bargain store.

"No," she replied. "You misunderstand. You help me and all, but you do it out of duty, not out of love, and I can't blame you none. I wasn't much of a mother to you or a role model for anyone. But knowing I'm dying soon puts a different spin on how I live my last days."

Marty had never had a son and her grandchild was denied her. She later told me, "When I saw Miguel, he looked like a little lost boy. My heart wanted to help him find his way." And he did not shy away from her, for reasons of his own. They babbled away in Spanish while I felt like a stepchild.

Leaving them to talk, I went looking for the nurse to learn more about Miguel's prognosis. When I stepped into the corridor, I saw two men about fifty feet away, standing near the nurse's station talking. I would have sworn the one with his back to me was Mr. Guzman. The other one was unmistakably Mexican Joe.

The nurse's station was located at the corner of two intersecting corridors. As I cautiously approached it, my Reeboks made the squeaking noise that rubber shoes make on tile. The man facing me looked up. He quickly said something to the man with his back to me, and then they both hurried off in opposite directions.

I ran to the nurse's station and screeched to a stop. I looked both ways in the intersecting corridors, saw neither man but ran in the direction Mexican Joe went, rounded a corner holding on to its edge, and almost toppled over a medicine cart.

Apologizing profusely, I kept running.

"Stop," yelled an authoritative voice behind me.

I stopped and turned to face hospital security.

By the time I showed my ID, told a tale about sighting an illegal alien, and was let go, I had no chance of finding either man. Still, I kept walking and looking and hoping. At the end of the next corridor, I turned to the right. The hospital chapel was at the corridor's end. I had visited it frequently after Shaun was born, hoping the irrevocably true right answer as to what I should do would come to me with divine inspiration. Marty said it didn't. From day one, the day she learned I was pregnant, Marty said Shaun would be better off being adopted by strangers than he would be in the hands of "those Philistines," that's actually what she called the Roses. As it turned out, she knew more about them than I did. She certainly knew more about what it would take to raise a child and she didn't let me forget it.

Marty had me when she was a few months older than I was when I had Shaun. "I wasn't much of a mother," she said often enough. And it was true. She didn't cast a large enough shadow to color in the lines marked "motherhood."

"But I *was* a mother," she always added.

Marty's unspoken insinuation was that I never even tried to be a mother. And it too was true. I condemned her for casting a slim shadow, then walked in the same sun and cast no shadow at all.

But the time for casting shadows was past for Marty and me; at least for her child named Miriam and my child named Shaun. Marty and I did what we did. Now I'm doing what I have to do. And, may God let us outlive our regrets.

I went into the chapel feeling instant remorse for the decision I made in there sixteen years before, when I decided Shaun would be better off living with his father. I felt betrayed. The inspiration I thought I'd had had not been divine. Now I just wanted to get on with my life and I couldn't do it until I finished my mission to impose biblical justice for Shaun's death.

Even though I didn't acknowledge it to him at the time, I did hear what Billy Rose said when we had our argument. I also heard what he didn't say. He didn't say, "You can't bring Shaun back." He didn't say, "You abdicated your right to parental rage when you gave up the duties of parental responsibility." And he didn't say, "It was Shaun, himself, who'd bought the drugs that killed him."

He didn't say those things because Billy Rose was fighting for something that meant as much to him as what I was fighting for meant to me. But Billy Rose did not want to alienate me and he knew the issue of Shaun would. So we were fighting against each other this time, and not the world. It was a fight he didn't have a chance of winning. It was a fight I had already lost.

I sat in the last pew of the chapel, the door at my back. I breathed in deeply, let it out.

Then something cold and round pressed against the back of my neck.

The steel barrel of a gun.

"Let it go," a voice said. The same voice I had heard a few nights before, floating down from atop a ridge, but this time without an accent.

"You can get hurt snooping in my business," he said. "Let it go."

I started to turn to look behind me.

"Don't," he said.

"I already know what you look like," I said. "Besides you won't shoot me in here."

He sighed. "Normally not. But desperate people sometimes do desperate things, in desperation."

I sat still.

He removed the gun.

I didn't turn around.

"You're smart enough to understand when I say that getting involved with me can get you killed. Let it go, *Migra*."

"How do you know Enrique Guzman?" I asked.

The thud of the chapel door closing was my only answer.

HASTA MAÑANA

I jumped up, ran to the door, pushed it open, and looked both ways.

The corridor was empty.

CHAPTER EIGHTEEN

Mrs. MacMartin met me at the door of Miguel's room exuding unrestrained joy. "How did you find her?" she asked.

A fiftyish frump with upper middle class breeding, Mrs. MacMartin married a man much older than she was. When he retired, they moved to Arizona. She felt she needed to "keep making a contribution to society." She was the hospital psychologist.

I had searched the hospital for more than an hour hoping I'd see Mr. Guzman, but I had not found him. I hadn't found anyone else either, so Mrs. MacMartin's question confounded me as much as her grinning did. She was the shortest person in the room but her enthusiasm boosted her up to ten feet tall.

"How did I find who?"

"*Tia Martina,*" she exclaimed, "Miguel's Aunt Martina." With one hand she clasped her ample bosom. With the other she possessively clutched Miguel's file.

While Mrs. MacMartin's body nearly hummed with excitement, I choked on a few false starts, trying to get my bearings.

"Miguel's Aunt Martina?" I hadn't been gone *that* long. Who the hell was Miguel's Aunt Martina?

Marty smiled at me. As soon as I saw the look on her face, I knew she was playing one of the games she used to play with Uncle Connie and my other "uncles" when she became what they needed their woman to be. In the hour or so I had been gone, Marty had become Miguel's *Tia Martina.*

HASTA MAÑANA

"Wasn't she a dear?" Marty gushed at the psychologist, who appeared to take whatever Marty had told her at face value, or she was just so glad to find someone to claim Miguel she dismissed any questions that arose.

Marty grabbed a chunk of my arm with her fingers. "Miss Valencia brought me to see *mi* Miguel." She squeezed my arm as she had done when I was a child and she sensed I was on the verge of spilling her secrets. But what disturbed me were the tears welling up in her eyes when she spoke of Miguel. I could ignore her ranting and raving; I could overlook her cussing and fussing; I could accept her lies. But I could not stand to see her cry.

"*¿Cómo arregla quearon vos con él?*" I whispered. Marty had planned something and I wanted to know what it was.

"Oh, you don't have to speak Spanish," Marty warned. "Mrs. MacMartin speaks both languages fluently."

How stupid of me. She would have to speak Spanish to be Miguel's psychologist; he did not speak or understand English. But I had not expected to return to the room and be conscripted into a real life conundrum, so I was not thinking fast on my feet, a potentially lethal state to be in if you're in Marty's world.

My thinking agility quickly returned as I read the picture before me. Marty was standing with her arm linked through Miguel's, who was looking at her with the joyful expectation of a young boy looking at Santa Claus. Mrs. MacMartin was beaming like she had just won the trophy for the catch of the day.

I held up my hands as a disclaimer. "I cannot be involved in this," I said and started to back out of the room. "Under the circumstance, I should not even know about it. In fact, as someone who works for Immigration, I probably shouldn't have come here at all."

I was rambling, but if it got me out of the room and away from the mess brewing in Marty's meddling pot, I didn't care.

Turning to Mrs. MacMartin I said, "I'm sure you understand."

Turning to Marty I said, "I'll wait for you outside."

Turning to Miguel I nodded my head. All this was his fault. Here I was feeling sorry for him and what did it get me? Inside of an hour he'd stolen my mother, acquired an American relative, and if Marty had her way, more benefits would ensue.

Behind Miguel's big, round, little boy eyes and bewildered expression of desperation, he must have been laughing at my expense. *La Migra, su guasango.*

Indeed, I did feel very much the fool.

Marty spoke first. "You're right," she said. "We're not breaking any laws or anything but you should stay out of it. It might be one of those interest conflicts."

She'd already thought this out.

I looked at Miguel who nodded vigorously. A grin covered his face. He didn't understand a word she was saying, but he intrinsically trusted her with his future. I thought that odd since I was still having trouble trusting her with my past.

I walked away wondering what law I'd just broken, would knowingly or unknowingly break tomorrow, or the next, to help Marty keep the smile she had on her face at that moment, and the light of the angels shining in her eyes.

Back in the car I called the station in Nogales. I'd think of something to say if Mr. Guzman answered the phone. The relief of knowing he had not been in the hospital with Mexican Joe would cause something coherent to materialize.

HASTA MAÑANA

Mr. Poteat, of the East Texas Poteats, answered the phone. "Guzman's at a meeting," he said. "What can I do you for?"

"You can give me a number where I can reach him," I said.

"Why?" he asked. "He stand you up or something?"

"You got a nose problem or something, Mr. Poteat?"

"No, but I do got something you want."

I sighed. Games. Everybody wanted to play fuckin' games and that was literally the game Mr. Poteat wanted to play, as he made clear on every possible occasion.

The only way to get rid of Mr. Poteat was to talk dirty and there was nothing dirtier than threatening him with a Journeyman on his case. "I need to give Mr. Guzman some information he asked for, asshole. Do you want to be the one to delay him getting it?"

"In that case, Miss Valencia," he sweetly said, "he left here going to the Tucson office. If he's not there, I don't know where he is."

I hung up without thanking him, unlocked the passenger side of the car so Marty could get in, and went back into the hospital to again search the corridors.

"Where the hell have you been?" Marty asked when I returned to the car twenty minutes later. "Don't you know it's hot out here?"

"Don't you know I could turn you in for whatever you're planning to do?"

"You'd have to know what it was first," she laughed. "Anyway you wouldn't do that. I'm your mother."

"You didn't seem to remember that DNA tidbit back in the hospital, Miss Sanchez."

"Oh, that's what's got your panties up your crack," she said. "You wouldn't understand."

I looked at her and shook my head. I didn't have the heart to tell her the little scheme would not work.

I underestimated Marty's thespian talents. As we sat scorching in the car, Martina Anna-Maria Sanchez (she conveniently left out Valencia) was being inked in Miguel Antoine Sanchez-Figueroa's file as a stateside relative.

And once the first domino of governmental inaccuracy falls, it is hard to stop the wave.

CHAPTER NINETEEN

Earlier when I saw Mr. Guzman and Mexican Joe standing by the nurse's station, my stomach grumbled like two old men disagreeing. Now my intestines were coiled around themselves like a bed of snakes copulating in spring.

After a slow start and a bad beginning, I had finally regained some control over my life. So long as I stayed in my little garden apartment in Ventura del Sol and went to my non-threatening job teaching kindergarten, I had no surprises, no gotchas, and that was fine with me. But since I decided to have it out with Mexican Joe, control of my life had left me faster than last night's dinner topped off with prunes for dessert.

Marty, Billy Rose, Mr. Guzman, the Border Patrol, Mexican Joe, illegals, armadillos crossing the highway with their own state-made right-of-way signs, now had more control over my life than I did. At that moment, nothing would have given me more pleasure than to take Marty home and leave her all giddy and psyched up on helping her new found "nephew." But first I'd have to suffer through her exuberance during the drive all the way to Rio Rico, sixty kilometers away.

While we waited for the air conditioner to cool the car, I promised myself I would have no part in Marty's scheme. I would not even let her tell me what she planned.

Fat chance.

As soon as the car was comfortable to sit in, she blabbed what she and Miguel were going to do when he had day passes to leave the hospital with her. Never mind she hardly had energy enough to dress herself, and couldn't drive a car.

"You haven't forgotten I'm a Border Patrol Agent, have you?"

"What's that got to do with anything?" her innocent voice asked. "They know he came here illegally. They gave him medical asylum until he's better. All I'm doing is giving him a family so he can have a taste of normality once in a while."

"But you're pretending to be his aunt."

"That's not a crime," she said. "Seems to me like you called a few men uncle in your time and none of them were blood related to you, either. Anyway," she continued, "we're all God's children. We're only talking about day passes for now. He will be in therapy for a long time."

I could see her mind working as clear as you can see the gears turning in a fob watch with no back.

"A long time," she repeated. "Longer than I'll live. And who knows, in a few weeks I might need someone to stay with me round the clock, what with you working rotating shifts and putting in overtime, it might not be wise for me to depend on you too much."

Marty smiled.

My career flashed before my eyes. My badge. My shield. My gun. My legal cover to pursue Mexican Joe was flying out of the window propelled by a sick woman's need to be a real mother before she died.

Funny, I didn't hesitate when it came to the woman in the tunnel the night before, even though I knew saving her life would allow the baby to be born on American soil, thus bestowing citizenship on the child. But Miguel was not a helpless baby. He was seventeen, the same age as Shaun.

He was just a young boy trying to do a foolish thing and got caught in the worst way and it cost him his life. No, I mean it cost his family their lives.

I was getting confused. Was I thinking about Miguel or Shaun? Then I realized they were not so different. Both boys grew up too fast. Both tried something new for the first time, and once was enough to forever change their lives. Only Miguel survived the experience and Shaun didn't.

I breathed in a perfectly normal breath but I couldn't swallow it and I couldn't spit it out. I grabbed my throat, tried to massage the muscles into action.

Before that moment, all I had recognized in Miguel was a distraught young man, devastated by the brutal loss of his loved ones. But now my heart saw what Marty had immediately seen. Shaun. Not Shaun in the flesh but Shaun in age, Shaun in dreams, Shaun in daring.

I looked at Marty. She knew I now saw it, too. We lost a boy. We found a boy.

"You don't have to have a child to love a child." She grabbed my hand. "All those years you pretended Shaun was not your son," she said. "Calling this boy my nephew can't be any more wrong than that was."

She was quiet a minute, and then she spoke. "On second thought, what I want to do is more right. I'm giving this boy hope. Maybe the plan won't work, but hope will keep him alive until his own will returns to him."

She shook her head, looked away to a picture I could not see. "Nobody ever told you, did they? Shaun grew up like you did, on his own. I'm not blaming you; he was with his own father. That man was a real son of a bitch."

The vehemence with which Marty added the last part made me suddenly realize she knew something I had never told her. But she had said nothing all these years and she said nothing now.

"Thanks to my own failings, I was never given a chance with your boy, Shaun. Never saw him again after you left town." She didn't pretend a rush of grief when she said it, she just kept right on talking. "I had to read about him dying in the obits just like everybody else. I've been given a second chance to do what's right," she added. "It may shorten my days, but I'm going to take that chance and do something good this time."

Her words brought tears to my eyes and air to my lungs, air as pure and sweet as a newborn baby's breath. I grabbed Marty and held her close to me. By reaching out to Miguel, she was being more of a mother to me than she had been my whole life. She was showing me the unselfishness of love, how to sacrifice everything like mothers do countless times a day, day in and day out, never considering the cost.

She wanted to leave me a legacy of maternal love because one day I might need a role model again; next time I would have the right example.

Marty hugged me tight and kissed away my tears. My mother loved me. My heart felt as light as a *mariposa* in flight.

I had to tell her. I pulled away. "You know I can't help you, don't you?"

"I know," she whispered. "No more than you help your neighbor, Mrs. Kim."

"But I don't help her, "I said. "I don't even know what she's doing."

"And that's the way it will be with us," she reassured me.

It was plain to see. In her heart, Marty saw herself as a mother first, for the very first time in her life. And the light of that mission made her eyes clearer than I had ever before seen them.

When I looked into her beautiful face, her pain softened now by thoughts of helping Miguel, it was not obvious how hard her body was struggling to do its job.

And nothing about her attitude told me she had mere weeks to live.

CHAPTER TWENTY

Lying in wait is a routine part of every Border Patrol Agent's duties. Sometimes we get ensconced in a tight spot like a fat tick burrowed in a dog's ear and stay there for what seems like hours. We don't move, we don't talk except by occasional hand signals, we don't do anything but breathe, try to stay alert, and forget that our bodies have to empty out everything we put in.

Other times, we wait only a few minutes before confiscating fifty kilos of coke, three hundred pounds of marijuana, or apprehending thirty-five illegals.

Lying in wait requires patience, concentration, and determination. But most of all, lying in wait reinforces optimism. If we are in the right place and wait long enough, what we are looking for will come.

Neither Billy Rose nor Marty have either patience or optimism. They would have given up this quest to find Mexican Joe by now, they've said as much to me. They've done as much, too. They go for days without asking about my progress in finding Mexican Joe, or even mentioning Shaun by name.

Shaun was an illusion to Marty. A collage of images, scraps of data she collected from the newspapers: making the honor roll in Mrs. Frank's third grade class, playing soccer in junior high, protesting land development with other students in high school. But she never knew him face to face. Though his dying did disturb her, it did not make her disturbed. Oddly, Billy Rose reacted to Shaun's death by running away. He didn't even go to the funeral. He just disappeared as though he had stepped into a sinkhole, resurfaced several months later on the other side of the world, then caught a Singapore Airlines flight home. But when he returned his grieving was over.

I was the only one in an emotional time warp. Yet, strangely, I wasn't wallowing in pulsating grief so much as I was mired in the abstract fullness of loss. There was always going to be time to make up for lost time. Time to set things straight. Always time to work everything out. Abruptly there was no time for anything. Now my time is filled with fantasies about how I'm going to get rid of Mexican Joe.

My sightings of Mexican Joe increased after the night on the hilltop, but I saw him in inconvenient places; inconvenient for me, convenient for him, as though he chose the time and place. As though he was the one looking for me. Would he end up killing me the way he did Shaun? No. He couldn't do that, he couldn't give me tainted drugs unless he forced them into my veins, and I didn't believe that was his style.

As I climbed higher into the mountain, I told myself the sun must be getting to me, making me stupid. To even think the things I was thinking, I must be delusional.

It was Friday morning. I was hiking in the area where Mr. Guzman and I had seen Mexican Joe. When I started out, the early morning sky had been slightly overcast, the air smelled of wet sage and damp earth from the previous night's rain. But that was helpful. It is easier to find prints after a rain. Then even Styrofoam shoes, sometimes worn to mask shoe tracks, leave a discernable imprint.

This would be a good day. I would will it so. I was looking in the right place. Mexican Joe wouldn't be in

Effrain Canyon where many illegals jump the fence and make a mad dash across I-19 to the U.S. side. It was much too visible and risky for someone who knew his or her way around the Border Patrol. A tactical maneuver Mexican Joe must have mastered, since he had never been apprehended and was not known to FBI, DEA, or INS.

See, Mr. Guzman, I thought. I don't need you to tell me what to do. I might be a novice compared to you, but I have common sense. Way back when Billy Rose first gave me the name and description, I had the police check records to see if Mexican Joe fit the description of any known drug smuggler.

I laughed at myself for talking to myself. Again I said it must be due to the heat. But I also laughed because I hadn't thought about Mr. Guzman since I'd seen him in the hospital, if I did in fact see him. And, under the circumstances, I should have thought about him. He had been accused of stealing drugs from the Miami Police Department evidence room. Mexican Joe was a drug smuggler. Doubt began to creep into my foresworn resolve not to read anything into the allegation against Mr. Guzman other than what I knew to be true.

Between huff and puffs, I climbed and sweated and told myself I could always ask Mr. Guzman if he had been in Tucson General Hospital at four-thirty on the twenty-fifth of June. He could always say, "Yes, no, or go to hell." But I assured myself that the way he responded would tell me more than his words.

By ten o'clock, I began to tire. I had followed a circuitous route, which meandered through the mountains as well as on flat land. The inaccessibility of the trail, the rugged terrain, and the proximity to the border made it ideal for smugglers. And like any other hiker or smuggler, as the case sometimes was, I was dressed in khaki shorts, Timberland hiking boots, and carrying a backpack with water, sandwich, and a first aid kit. The difference? I carried my gun and ID inside the pouch strapped around my waist and I wasn't sure where they carried theirs.

We practiced lying in wait at the Academy. We'd stay out in the field for hours at night with swarms of mosquitoes sounding quaint music, syncopated by croaking frogs. We stayed out during the day, lying in sand with temperatures over a hundred degrees and chiggers and sand gnats feasting on our sun-roasted skin.

"The sand is your friend," the Academy instructors drilled into our heads. "The sand is your friend."

Out in the desert, I guess the sand is a friend, especially when the rocks are hot enough to cook an egg and the sagebrush is so dry you can blow it away with a mere sneeze. Because if you dig deep enough the sand is cool; ask any animal that cannot stand the heat of day. Yet, there are animals who like to bask in the sun.

I was reliving my Academy days, recalling names of desert plants and animals, when a flash of color caught my eye. About a meter to the right of the trail lay a multi-colored strand. Excitement spewed through me like a geyser.

Omygod. An old Indian necklace, maybe dating from antiquity, lay right in my path. I envisioned it behind a protective glass in a museum with an "On Loan From" with my name on it.

I bent down and picked up the necklace and as I did, the opposite end turned back on itself to reveal a head. I was holding the tail of a Gila monster, one of only two poisonous lizards in the world. The scales are colored like Indian beadwork. My mistake.

Every nerve ending in my body froze. Thankfully my mind replayed a little ditty from my Academy days:

> The hot, shifting sand is my friend.
> Tarantulas aren't poisonous to men.
> Gila monsters won't bite unless provoked.
> God save me if I'm wrong. Amen.

Slowly bending my knees, arm still outstretched like it was when I first picked up the Gila monster, I gently put it down and backed away.

"*Buena, La Migra.*"

Mexican Joe's voice was as clear to my ears as the skittering lizard was to my eyes. A quick look around told me no one was there but me.

A shadow passed over me. Suddenly in the middle of a desert heat wave I felt chilled. Death was the only company I knew that came so silently. I looked up and saw two vultures, circling low. Were they for me? Could they smell death even before it occurred?

"*La Migra. Venga.*" Come to me.

The voice laughed now, mocked me. His ridicule challenged me to action. Without considering the consequences, I quickly followed.

The outcropping of rocks I climbed grew wide and the land uneven. Despite the heavy feeling in my heart that something terrible waited for me around the next outcropping, I persevered through the sand and the heat. The land went down, I went down with it, following the nagging voice. What else could I do? The voice was ahead by only a few feet. It assaulted my ears as surely as my hot breath parched my throat.

The vultures circled, wide and low, stopped, swooped down.

I desperately needed a drink of water from my backpack. I could not stop for fear the voice would outdistance me.

The desert is an arid sauna and we carry extra water to keep our fluid levels in check. Of course, I was the agent who got yelled at for giving water to illegals when I apprehended them and they were severely dehydrated like I was now starting to feel. But what else could you do when you encountered people with cracked lips and throats parched so badly they could barely speak?

"You can't afford to give away your water," I was told.

"You might need it for yourself," Billy Rose said, so I started carrying extra water in my vehicle, and food, too.

"You just encourage them if you give them water," was the closest anyone would come to forbidding me to do it. No one made me stop, but no one was happy about it either, except maybe the illegals.

I followed the voice and when the rocks kissed the desert floor down the far side of the hill I'd climbed earlier, the laughing stopped. I looked right, then left, and quickly back right. I saw movement, or at least I thought I did. I unsnapped the pouch nestled close to my tummy and took out my gun. But it was a wasted motion. The man lying on the ground before me, lips swollen and blistered, was so weak he could barely move. I looked up, saw the vultures hovering, lying in wait.

God forgive me. I was glad they waited for him and not for me.

His name was Pedro. He said he was from Culiacán and he had hitched rides with friends, strangers, on trucks and trains, to get to Sonora where he met up with a guide and a group of others wanting to cross the border. They had walked a circuitous route for two days, paralleling the border, looking for the right place, waiting for the right time to cross. He was trying to get to North Carolina. His son could get work for him there on a pig farm.

When I found Pedro, he had propped himself upright against a rock. If he lay down, he said, he would be unrolling the welcome mat for death to step in. It was one hundred and ten degrees and he was wearing every piece of clothing he owned, which made him sweat even more and probably cooled him down some, yet it quickened his dehydration. His feet were swollen around the sandals he wore. His eyes saw things that were not there and held no hope or dreams.

Pedro was disoriented but he understood when I told him I was a Border Patrol Agent and I would radio for help. While we waited for the EMTs, I gave him water and a quarter of a sandwich, just enough not to make him sick. Then he seemed to need to talk, in case no one else ever got the chance to know his story.

I let him tell it.

Pedro said he had been traveling with a group of people, which steadily decreased in number as stragglers dropped out as they walked and climbed and walked some more. When he had fallen ill, the scout had told him to stay behind, but he promised he could keep up and he had for a while. Then late last night, when they had gone single file through a pass, the scout told him to go last, instead of first as he had been doing. Pedro made it through the pass but he never saw his group again. The scout cut him out and left him, like animals leave the sick and injured to die.

The EMTs came before Pedro told me how he finally made it across the border. They airlifted him out. He would stay in the infirmary three or four days, then be returned to Mexico.

I didn't think Pedro would try to make the trip again.

HASTA MAÑANA

What can be an adventure, a challenge for you at twenty-five, can be a nightmare at sixty, when your life expectancy is not many more years than that.

"Angel, Verde," he whispered as they took him away. Green Angel. *"Nunca te olvidaré."* I will never forget you.

When I later told the story to Marty, I said Mexican Joe must have seen Pedro dying but was afraid to get help. When he saw me, he called out to me, then taunted me, daring me, knowing I would chase after him and find Pedro instead.

Marty had a more ethereal explanation. "Pedro was lying in wait for you," she said. "Your spirit guide led you to save Pedro's life so one day Pedro can save yours."

I believed Marty was having flashbacks to a very bad trip until I met Pedro the second time.

CHAPTER TWENTY-ONE

When I got up at five o'clock Sunday morning to get ready for work, Billy Rose had not returned from his business trip. He was twelve hours overdue, but he'd been late several times before when he had delivered customized computer programs to his clients and "bugs," he never explained what they were, had gotten into the system.

The phone rang while I was in the shower. I didn't make an effort to get it until the answering machine picked up and I heard Billy Rose's voice. Then I grabbed a towel, but streaked naked to the phone, leaving water prints where I stepped. Unfortunately he had changed answering machines again and I couldn't figure out how to make the damn thing stop so I could talk. "I have to fumigate some bugs," he said through the answering machine. "I'll be here a few more days tweaking the software." Tweaking was his euphemism for you wouldn't understand even if I explained so I won't.

I wrapped the oversized towel around me and started to dry off.

Then Billy Rose's tone became warm, intimate. "I'm giving you more notice this time, Miriam. Please go with me to Guadalajara in two weeks." He paused, as one does collecting one's thoughts or broaching a difficult subject. Then he continued. As he talked, I could imagine his face under a lot of circumstances I had previously witnessed, but none fit the emotion in his voice now when he said, "Everything I've done has been for you and me. Why don't you forget about Mexican Joe and marry me like we always planned? We belong together. It's time we started having fun again. Don't you remember how it used to be?"

While Billy Rose paused I thought, *Of course I remember how it used to be.* But that was then and this is now. When things change, rarely do they ever go back to the way they were. If his constant focus weren't himself, he might see it, too.

Through the answering machine, his breathing sounded like shallow echoes in a deep well. His voice, hurled at me through time and space and distorted by electronic gadgetry broke and cracked. "I am so sorry," he said. "But nothing I can do will bring him back to you."

Then he hung up.

I replayed his message a second time before I was distracted by a news bulletin on TV. The volume was so low I could barely hear what was said, but I did hear mentioned sixty kilos of cocaine.

Initially, I thought the newscast was a local story because Border Patrol Agents have cross-designations with the DEA and U.S. Customs. Drugs and other illegal contraband confiscated by our agents contribute to their numbers being as high as they are. Since I had been off work for about three days, had not talked to anyone from the facility for two, and had not read the newspapers, I wouldn't have known if we had been involved in something really big.

When the volume of the television was turned up, I discovered the broadcast was a national news story. The feature was about the New Jersey State Police stopping a tractor-trailer full of produce. The load had originated in Sonora, Mexico and was headed for New York City via one of the state's major thoroughfares.

The truck's driver, a Hispanic male, and his Hispanic

male passenger had apparently broken no laws, but were stopped by the State Police anyway. Both men had proper identification and resident alien cards permitting them to live, travel, and work anywhere in the U.S. By the time I got up to speed on what was going on, the lawyer for the trucking firm was saying, "The driver was stopped because of racial profiling." It was common knowledge the New Jersey Turnpike law enforcement officers had been accused of profiling for years.

"The illegal stop," the lawyer said, "led to an illegal search, which led to the discovery of the drugs." He implied that anybody could have put the drugs in the truck. The cocaine couldn't be used as evidence in a court trial anyway, he said, because of the illegal way in which it was discovered.

The lawyer for the driver said, "My client drove the truck, he did not load it. All he knew about what was in the truck was what the bill of lading specified. Since NAFTA," he continued, "his truck sits in lines ten miles long for indeterminable amounts of time, approaching the border. By the time the trucks finally cross, some of them may have drugs or people stowed in, under, and on them, simply because the lines crossing the border are moving at a snail's pace. But the only thing my client is guilty of doing is what he was paid to do, and that was drive the truck. He was a good driver with no outstanding violations. The only reason he was stopped was because of racial profiling."

The reporters all spoke at once, asking questions, prodding for more information, whether speculative or not. The lawyer went into a spiel about presumptive intimidation, how these were Mexican nationals accustomed to a police force that is sometimes indistinguishable from the criminal element and how his client, playing out that scenario in his head, had presumed the worse and panicked.

Then I listened in disbelief to the rest of the story.

"In his confused and frightened state," the lawyer said, "my client attempted to run across six lanes of high speed traffic outside of Newark, New Jersey." The lawyer looked pained when he said, "Of course, not being familiar with the area, he didn't realize that if he made it past the high speed traffic, he wasn't going very far once he landed in the marshes." Then he glared into the cameras. "But the police certainly did."

And indeed the driver hadn't gone far. He was shot thirteen times in the back before he got to the white line in the road.

It was only after the driver was killed that the cache of cocaine was discovered in with the lettuce. To many, that made it a "righteous" shooting, in retrospect.

The story held me captive for several reasons. First, it seemed to me to be an overuse of firepower to stop a man running toward real estate that offered no escape, except maybe being sucked to his death in the marsh. And I felt like a traitor to the brotherhood of law enforcement officers for feeling that way because I knew the police in question would be crucified for their actions by the media and by every civil rights group with even a tangential reason to be irate. Officers not even remotely involved would be under close scrutiny from John Q. Public and I didn't envy them that. When the Border Patrol made the papers in a negative way, I become anxious about my personal safety while in uniform for weeks after.

Second, the sheer volume of trucks crossing the southern border is problematic. The Border Patrol does not inspect them; that is the U.S. Customs Inspector's job. But even with specially trained dogs to help, theirs is an impossible task. For every vehicle that is apprehended with ninety-six illegal aliens stuffed in it or with the extra gas tank filled with drugs, undocumented numbers of vehicles get through. There just isn't the manpower to frisk every truck crossing the border. It takes a lot of time to check those with high profiles, so the lawyer was right in saying crossing the border is at a snail's pace.

The third reason the news item held my attention? Our close proximity to the Mexican border and the innumerable times certain scenarios have played out, we, too, use profiling to apprehend illegal aliens. Old, unattended cars or trucks, which are stranded along the highway with no apparent problems, sometimes have keys hidden under the front mat or under a rock a few paces away, and they are there waiting for their passengers to cross the border. Taxis and passenger vans are other high profile vehicles, especially if they are jam packed with people, or if feet are sticking up in the windows and no heads are in sight.

The last reason the news item caught my attention was because the incident happened on the East Coast and Billy Rose was just then talking to me via the answering machine from the East Coast. Admittedly, it is a huge area of the country, but you know how the mind makes free-form associations. Regrettably, those free-form associations distracted me and I missed a significant component of the news item. Two weeks passed before I learned the drugs confiscated in the incident were stolen from the police evidence room later in the day.

Once Billy Rose was on my mind that morning, I remembered our last day together and purely because I wanted to know, I pushed star-six-nine on the off-chance I could get the number from the phone he had used.

Thankfully he hadn't used his cell phone. I dialed the

number and it was answered by the desk clerk at a hotel in Linden, New Jersey, which is just across the river from New York City, where Billy Rose had headed.

Yes, William Joseph Rose was registered. No, the desk clerk said, she couldn't connect me to his room because Mr. Rose had left explicit instructions not to be disturbed before ten a.m. By now her tone held an attitude unmistakable to another woman. It was then only nine-fifteen, she concluded, and hung up without asking if I wanted to leave a message. She probably—no, she definitely—had her eyes on Billy Rose. His curly blond hair and lanky body adorned in expensive clothes attracted a certain kind of woman. From her tone, there was no doubt in my mind she had already moaned his name between the sheets and was now feeling quite possessive.

I arrived at work a half-hour early that morning. The sun was up, yet the air was still cool. Working days again felt like a treat. My circadian rhythms would be normal for thirty days, but for now, butterflies tickled my stomach as I cautiously awaited the start of my new assignment working with a new journeyman. It was Sale Day in Nogales. Originally, I had been assigned to work downtown with Mr. Molloy. First thing after muster, I learned Mr. Molloy had been reassigned to night shift and that Mr. Guzman would continue as my journeyman for the next rotation. I should have been surprised, but frankly, I wasn't. By then I knew Mr. Guzman watched me as assiduously as I watched him. And in that case, working with him may be a good thing. I had wanted to ask him if he was with Mexican Joe in Tucson General Hospital late Thursday afternoon. Now I could ask him face to face.

Or at least I thought I would ask him. But what he said to me on the way to the garage to get our vehicles preempted all chances of that happening.

"This is not my idea of fun," he tersely said. "This rotation we'll play it strictly by the book. You don't talk about your personal life and I won't talk about mine." He got into his vehicle and headed toward downtown Nogales.

I later learned through radio communications that earlier the same morning, Mr. Guzman arrived at the station from out of town and had pulled in a few markers to be rotated to the day shift, then insisted he be assigned as my journeyman. The other agents razzed me for being so "special."

Secretly, I was flattered.

But if I had known the real reason Mr. Guzman went to all that trouble to be near me, I would have been scared to death.

CHAPTER TWENTY-TWO

The best thing about working days was, of course, my body being in sync with its twenty-nine-year-old pattern of sleeping and waking. The second best thing about working days was being able to enjoy the desert's full array of natural gifts.

Early in the morning, the air was crisp and cool. Later in the day, it was hot and dry.

If I had time before the shift got busy, I could stand on a ridge and relish the vibrant blooms of the paloverde trees shining golden yellow above the calm greens and browns of greasewoods and mesquites. I could watch a mother gambol quail and her chicks furiously scratch for breakfast. I could squint against the sun coming at me from New Mexico and pretend the shimmering vertical pipes clustered in the valley below were really theater organs readying to serenade me, and not just prickly cacti waiting to ribbon my uniform when I chased illegals through them.

Some days the slowest and fastest, the giant tortoise and the spirited roadrunner of cartoon fame, were revealed to me. Other days, I might see a gopher pop his head out of a hole, or a large scorpion tuck his claws in and curl back his tail so he looked like a rock.

But I didn't get to see any of those things on Sale Day because I was confined to downtown Nogales, which consists of four blocks, including the port of entry where walk-through traffic on Sale Day is three to four thousand more than usual.

CAROLYN WILKERSON

On Sale Day, downtown Nogales is blocked off to vehicular traffic and the area takes on a circus atmosphere, with music blasting from the tops of buildings, announcers trying to talk over the crowds on loudspeakers, and food kiosks with fiery cayenne and cilantro delectables for the palate. Merchants move to the sidewalks to peddle their wares and hire spotters to stand atop tall ladders to look for shoplifters. The local police are unusually busy and if there is a problem with illegals, they do not hesitate to call us. That's how I met Jorge Beltran.

Mexicans who live in towns along the U.S. border may be eligible for passes, allowing them to cross the border for up to seventy-two hours, and they can travel up to twenty-five miles into the interior. Those who have cars can get a drive-out sticker. Many Mexicans come to Nogales on Sale Day legally. Because the crowds are so large, many also come illegally. Some work in the shops on Sale Day, illegally, of course, but the Indian, Korean, and Russian shopkeepers see the expediency in using Mexican salespeople when most of the clientele will be Mexican, like it is on Sale Day.

Since I've now seen the scenario played out a few times, I've developed a theory about how the police came to know Jorge was here illegally. At the time, though, it was a mystery because he was a tall, lanky, clean-cut guy between sixteen and eighteen years old who didn't fit the obvious profile for an illegal. He was cock-sure, articulate in English, which he spoke with only a slight Spanish accent, and dressed the way the Americans were dressed.

I responded to the police call to pick up an illegal at the dress shop on Graves Street. When I arrived, a nice little argument was being waged in three languages as to what the problem really was. The police officer's side was the obvious one for me to take, and silently I did, though I let the other two parties have their say.

"No, no, no," the shopkeeper insisted. "I no hire illegal. I get trouble." He turned his back, tantamount, I suppose, to washing his hands of the whole mess.

A few people standing around took that as their cue to get involved. Several offered up goods allegedly sold to them by Jorge.

The shopkeeper couldn't see them to be impressed.

Jorge's story? He was a resident alien with a permanent resident alien card.

If that was true, he was both legal to be there and to work.

The problem? His card was in his coat pocket and his cousin had worn his coat where?

"To Mexico. Okay?"

As much as I knew Jorge wanted me to believe him, I didn't. His was a story I heard practically every day. The card was a document, like my badge, that you don't get casually separated from.

But I smiled and said, "Okay."

I steered him away from the shop and began to escort him to the transport vehicle.

He came willingly.

As we approached the vehicle, I said, "Give me your name, address, and birth date and I can run your card for you." I reassured him. "Everything will be just fine."

With the utterance of three small words, "run your card," the composed, well-spoken young man, whose stride had previously matched mine, developed feet of lead and lapsed into barely understandable Spanish. I told him to take a deep breath and calm down, I wasn't angry with him for losing his card.

The onlookers, grown to crowd status now, were behind us and didn't know what I had said, yet I would bet money many of them were illegal and were probably seeing themselves in his shoes. But I didn't look back and neither did Jorge. He was having too much trouble going forward. As we neared the transport vehicle, I reminded him everything would be okay as soon as I ran his card.

His composure wilted like a water-starved flower left in the sun too long. No longer able to put one foot in front of the other, Jorge stopped.

I stopped, too.

Jorge told me he had lied. He said he had crossed the border illegally on his cousin's card and had worked illegally at the dress shop from seven to two. "I do all the time," he said. "But today no count," he added. "He no pay."

"You worked seven hours and you didn't get paid?"

He shook his head. "No." Visibly unnerved, his voice broke, his English deteriorated. "No. Mr. Sung say he get especial trouble if he pay me."

I wondered why it took Mr. Sung all day long to remember he'd get into trouble hiring illegals. I asked Jorge, "How did the police know you were illegal?"

"Don't know. One minute is working hard, next minute Mr. Sung is talking to police. They come over and he tell me he can't pay 'cause I'm illegal."

It took only a few more answers for me to understand that Jorge didn't know he was supposed to be paid whether he got busted or not. I was so angry, fine hairs on the top of my head bristled. It was bad enough illegals were paid substandard wages under the table. Hell, that one fact probably accounted for half of the illegal crossings. But to have somebody work all day and not pay them anything at all was slave labor. In America, that is illegal even for illegal aliens.

At times, some of my duties cause me moral dilemmas, but on this issue I was clear. Jorge worked hard for seven straight hours. Jorge was going to get paid.

My attitude must have said I was going to use the gun I had my hand rested on as I stormed back toward the shopkeeper, Jorge in tow. A pathway opened for us.

The music stopped.

The loudspeaker announcer fell silent.

I was the only one who knew what was going to happen next. The shopkeeper was the only one who didn't seem to care.

The bristle had gone to my underarms, now. I was going to make damned sure he did care by the time I finished.

Mr. Sung said, "I no pay. I no hire illegal."

"Let me see your resident alien card."

He gave it to me.

"Why didn't you ask for Jorge's papers at seven o'clock this morning before you let him work?" I asked, and not very nicely. "That was the time for you to be concerned about legality."

"He say he okay. I believe."

"You know better than to take his word," I said. "And I know better than to take yours. Give the man his money."

I turned to Jorge. "How much did he promise you?"

"He promise fifty dollars for day," Jorge suddenly regained his composure. "Fifty dollars," he said to the crowd.

The crowd knew more poignantly than I did how much that was really worth across the border. They said, "Fifty dollars."

"You worked seven to two," I said to Jorge. "Did you get a break?"

"No."

"You're supposed to get a break if you work that long," I told him, "so let's just say you worked a full day." Turning back to the shopkeeper I said, "Give the man fifty dollars."

The shopkeeper continued to look at me, but made no indication he was going to part with fifty dollars.

"I'm not leaving here until he gets his money," I said. "He's not leaving here until he gets his money."

The crowd moved closer.

Mr. Sung wasn't impressed.

"But you might be the one who has to leave, especially if I recommend employer sanctions against you to the U.S. Attorney."

The crowded erupted into spontaneous applause.

Mr. Sung didn't respond, but he kept looking at his card being waved back and forth in his face. I hoped he was thinking logically. I had made a threat and I had to follow through. I decided to put it in dollars and cents.

"Since we've been standing here you've already lost five times fifty dollars, Mr. Sung. You understand that. What you don't seem to understand is, even if we catch a guy working illegally, he still deserves to get paid for the time he worked.

"The reason you're here, Mr. Sung, is the same reason forty-five hundred people walked though the port today, to have a chance to get something they can't get anywhere else in the world. This is my last warning, don't fuck this man out of his money."

I didn't know if he was shocked at such coarseness from a woman and decided to comply, or if he was going to shut me up once and for all.

He reached into the till. A lot of shop owners keep guns there.

My hand was resting on my holster. I unsnapped my gun

for easy access. The noise was loud. Obvious.

The crowd looked from me to him and back to me.

I don't know what Mr. Sung's intent was when he put his hand into the till. When he pulled it out, he clutched two twenties and a ten. He threw them at Jorge, who was not so incredulous that he didn't scoop them up before somebody else did.

"Thanks, man," he said jubilantly, then reconsidered, "I mean Ma'am."

I felt pretty good myself.

I had been right to insist that Jorge get paid. Illegals are taken advantage of all the time but they don't complain. They are used to having their rights violated back where they come from and don't realize that here they have legal rights whether they're American citizens or not.

At the same time, if Mr. Sung had held firm, his legal problems would have been minor. Employer sanctions are few and far between.

Mr. Sung knew that, too.

Still, the court of public opinion could have held him liable. Crowds can be unpredictable when their favorite doesn't win, and this crowd was clearly backing the long shot, Jorge, who proudly stuffed the money into the pocket of his jeans. He then got into the van to be taken to the facility, processed, and sent back to Mexico.

Jorge Beltran told me he crossed the border several times a week and had been caught fifty-six times. "Not as risky as working the streets back home," he said. "Where I come from, Latino boys sell their bodies to male tourist. I sneak across the border, but I no do that."

CHAPTER TWENTY-THREE

The upside of Sale Day? It lines the pockets of Nogales merchants with cash. The downside? It is a pain in the ass for law enforcement officials. What with drunken street fights, shoplifting, smuggling, and illegal crossings at all time highs, there are enough illegal and criminal activities to keep the Nogales Police, U.S. Customs agents, and the Border Patrol busy. Even the EMTs become involved.

The main duty of the Border Patrol Agent working transport is to pick up illegals, from other agents or the police, and transport them to the facility for processing, as I had done with Jorge earlier. After processing, illegals are taken back to their country. If you work at the southwest border, ninety percent of the time, Mexico is the home country. We escort them to the exit ports in Nogales. If there are no illegals for transport, the transport agent can help with arrests, if needed.

After leaving Jorge at the facility, I drove into the residential area surrounding downtown to check along the border fence where we know illegals sometimes jump into the U.S. On Sonoita Avenue, an eight- or nine-year-old-boy ran into the street in front of my van, frantically waving his hands above his head.

I slammed the brakes, rolled down the window, and yelled, "Are you crazy? I almost ran over you." My tone emanated more from knowing I barely missed hitting him than from actually being angry.

"They're in our back yard," he said in an excited

whisper. "My mother is scared but I'm not."

His mother ran out to the street. "The three illegals. They went back there." She pointed to the old wooden structure sitting back from the street in a small grove of trees.

The woman began to whisper her plea, speaking half in Spanish, half in English, saying, "They steal my clothes from the line, they sneak into my kitchen and eat our food off my table, they scare my children, and they rock my dogs, to chase them away."

Of course I knew she was talking cumulatively and not necessarily about what the illegals who had *just* gone through her yard had done. She lived a block from the huge storm drain where I helped the pregnant lady, only her house was high on a hill where the street curved back on itself, putting the house up over the drain. Illegals sometimes ran from the drain up to her yard, and then a scout could see them from a distance. They waited in the shack for a shuttle van or a taxi to come and pick them up. Agents complained about the shack, but couldn't get it torn down. Whenever possible, I drove by to check for activity.

I pulled into the woman's driveway, parked the van, and followed her to the edge of her backyard where she stopped and pointed. I continued walking to the abandoned shack, unholstered my gun and readied my Maglite flashlight to illuminate the inside of the shack, then knocked lightly on the door, like an illegal would.

No one answered.

There was a hole where the knob should have been. The door was held closed by a wire hanger attached to the door on one end. Someone with a small hand had reached through the hole and wrapped the other end around a nail affixed to the doorjamb. I slowly unraveled the wire, then pushed the old dilapidated door, which did not squeak, but clothes rustled inside, then there was a hushed whisper.

The shack was occupied.

Gun drawn, I sighted it down the barrel of the flashlight, which was pointed straight out in front of me. When the door was about three inches in, I kicked it the rest of the way and simultaneously flicked on the flashlight. The beam was so intense you'd swear it'd start a fire if held close to paper.

The door bursting open noise startled the illegals. They froze where they were, giving me the moment I needed to sweep the room with light and pick my mark. I pointed my weapon into their guide's eyes, blinding him with the light.

The guide growled at me. Said some things about my mother that once may have been true and, in an effort to get the light out of his eyes, flailed his arms as though having a seizure. I was glad I'd remembered that use of the flashlight from my Academy training, because there were not three illegals as the boy and his mother had told me. There were twelve. And the man who had smuggled them across was a big, smelly, mean-looking son of a bitch who probably would have jumped me if he hadn't been temporarily blind.

I handcuffed the guide while he was still disoriented and had the others file out to the van one by one. I drove them to the facility to be processed, then went back into the field. As soon as I turned left onto Mariposa Road, a call came through on my radio. Fifteen illegals crossed over to the east side of the freeway and had scattered in Crawford Canyon. Fifteen more were on the west side waiting to cross.

The fifteen that had already crossed would soon be lost to view in the abundant foliage of the poplars, junipers, and sycamores, so I concentrated on the fifteen waiting to cross. They had just jumped the border fence from Mexico into Effrain Canyon on the west side of I-19. They were waiting to run across I-19, jump the guardrail, and scatter like the others unless I stopped them first.

It wasn't possible to capture them on the west side of the freeway, where they were crouched down behind the guardrail, yet clearly visible on the camera, alerting us to their activity. If I drove down the embankment in the van with Border Patrol painted on it in foot high letters, they would see it and run back across the border, which was just behind them, hide until I left, and then cross again as soon as I was out of sight.

Not in a mood to play hide and seek, I drove up to the signal light, turned left onto I-19, went up the east side of the freeway, and pulled off onto the curb just before the steel guardrail started. I then drove the van down the embankment and parallel to the freeway until I reached a trampled and depressed patch of earth where the others jumped. I parked in the bushes below the guardrail, opened the side door of the van, and waited.

In about three minutes a body soared into the air over the guardrail. I saw the look of astonishment in his face when he looked down below his feet and saw me standing there, badge in the hand held high above my head, gun in the other hand.

By the time he landed on the ground, the futility of trying to run had been internalized. I pointed to the van. He got in, sat quietly, and waited with me.

The next one did the same. And the next. I started seating from the front near the wire partition, which separated driver from passengers. When the last illegal landed and took his seat, the van was full.

It was the easiest apprehension I've pulled off so far.

When I took the van full of illegals from the freeway to the facility, Mr. Guzman was already there. We arranged to meet at Tricky Wash for lunch.

Tricky Wash was a popular crossing for Nogales, Mexico residents who crossed the border for lunch at McDonald's or Denny's or one of the other fast food hot spots. Mr. Guzman and I parked our vans at the entrance to Tricky Wash and we sat in mine to eat lunch.

For the thirty minutes we sat there eating in silence, no one climbed over the fence. My theory was that a scout was somewhere out of our sight redirecting the crossing traffic around us, probably to the main port where the Sale Day crowds were still heavy.

In fact, some of the people approaching the main port from Mexico were so bold and brazen they banded together in a group and rammed through the entry gate like they were storming the Bastille. If enough went through at once, many invariably made it without getting caught.

After lunch, Mr. Guzman and I drove our vehicles to the port of entry and arrived just in time to see a group of six people on the Mexican side crouch like they were in a track meet, then run as fast as they could through the port. Three were stopped almost immediately upon touching American soil.

Two men and a woman got through the port and ran past our vans.

Mr. Guzman was parked behind me. When we jumped out of our vans and started chasing after them, he had a ten-yard lead on me.

The railroad line starts in Mexico and splits the town of

HASTA MAÑANA

Nogales into east and west as it travels north. Many illegals follow the tracks until they come to a customary load-up spot, a place where the train slows or stops, and they jump on, hitching a ride to the border. Of course, they chance being discovered when the train goes through Customs, so they get off, sneak through, around, or under the port, and jump back on before the train gets up speed again.

This day a train had cleared Customs and was starting to move when the six illegals rushed the port. The three that got away headed straight for the train yard, which had several tracks with cars on them waiting to go through Customs, and toward a train coming up the main track, picking up speed.

The three reached the main track before the train reached them. They stopped, looked back at us closing the gap, and then crossed the tracks. One later told us they were going to put the train between us and them, then jump on the train from the far side, rather than chance being pulled off this side.

When they jumped, Mr. Guzman turned on his radio to let me know they had crossed the tracks. He must have taken it as a personal affront and his adrenaline kicked in. He sprinted toward the tracks with unbelievable speed.

The train bore down, closer. With each step Mr. Guzman took, the train rolled over yards of track, shortening the distance between them.

The engineer blew the train's whistle, warning him.

Mr. Guzman ran faster.

The engineer blew the whistle again.

Ordinarily I would have sprinted too. Caught up to Mr. Guzman. Matched him step for step. Proved to him I was just as fast as he was. But as I gained on him, I saw a flash of movement out of the corner of my eye, near one of the stationary cars parked between the port and me. I turned my head.

Mexican Joe stood thirty feet away.

I stopped dead in my tracks, pulled my weapon, and sighted him down the barrel, right between his eyes. Gray-green eyes staring back at me without a trace of fear. From their expression they seemed the eyes of a friend.

It was unsettling.

Mexican Joe did not move.

This was the moment I'd envisioned every morning for the past five months. Every morning I'd wake up and say, "This is the day I'm going to kill Mexican Joe," and this day it would be true. He was in clear view, within shooting distance, and no one was close to him. All conditions were perfect. All I had to do was squeeze the trigger. Yet the force of his gaze drew me to him, shook my resolve to kill him and be done with it.

At the same time I thought all this, the anger deep inside me yelled, "Take the shot. A life for a life."

The engineer blew the whistle three times in rapid succession. The few people who had walked into the train yard looked toward the train, ignoring Mexican Joe and me. But that worked in my favor. All I had to do was squeeze the trigger and no one would hear the gun report over the train whistle blast. No one would see me kill him because the few people who were there were watching to see if the train splattered Mr. Guzman, bug on a windshield style, all over the track.

All I had to do was squeeze the trigger.

It was only a few seconds since I'd sighted Mexican Joe, but it seemed a lifetime ago that my mind ping-ponged between shoot and don't shoot.

HASTA MAÑANA

The engineer blew the whistle non-stop and the crossing signal clanged.

Out of the corner of my eye I saw Mr. Guzman jump the tracks.

My breath caught in my throat. I turned my head to look at him but closed my eyes so I wouldn't see.

A second later I opened my eyes and saw Mr. Guzman's black boots running alongside the train on the other side of the track. I sighed in relief and quickly looked back to Mexican Joe.

He wasn't there.

Deep in my soul, I sighed.

I holstered my weapon and again caught sight of Mr. Guzman's feet running along the other side the train. The woman he chased had fallen behind the two men. I could tell by her feet, she outdistanced Mr. Guzman by about ten yards, but he was quickly closing the gap.

"I'm too old for this shit," Mr. Guzman said, more to himself than to me. I don't think he knew his radio was still transmitting.

I laughed to relieve the tension that had built up inside of me, and then realized laughter was inappropriate for the circumstances. "I didn't think we were supposed to talk about personal stuff," I said.

But Mr. Guzman didn't hear the laughter or the words because he hadn't closed his microphone. He was huffing and puffing like a running back that had been benched all season and was suddenly sent out for a long one. The handheld radio was attached to his shirt near his shoulder, making it possible for me to hear every grunt and groan.

Just as I thought, *It's good I didn't jump the track. He would've had a heart attack if I'd outrun him,* his voice came through the radio again.

He said, "Oh, shit, God damn."

The emotion behind it filled me with dread.

He continued with, "She fell."

From his tone, there was no mistaking his meaning. My heart fell, too.

Try as I did, this time I could not close my eyes.

It is impossible to describe the horror of seeing a megaton train run over a person. The supreme blessing is that the weight of the train and the heat of the wheels neatly seals the wound, so there is little blood loss. It happens and it is over. The victim, her name was Ismelda, would have immediately gone into shock and then lost consciousness. But there were other injuries.

We later reconstructed events. When Ismelda jumped, she caught a handhold low on the side of the car and didn't have the strength or the quickness to pull up out of harm's way. One foot dragged on a railroad tie, pulled her down close to the track where her foot was run over by the train and amputated. That snatched her completely off the car, and the hand she had been holding on with was amputated when it hit the track. She then smashed her head on the railroad ties.

Fortunately EMTs were already in the area. They collected the severed extremities and covered the body before onlookers saw how bad it was mangled.

The EMTs assured Ismelda's traveling companions every effort would be made to reattach her hand and foot and sew up her head.

What they didn't tell them was that those would be cosmetic considerations for the family when they identified the body.

CHAPTER TWENTY-FOUR

When I was growing up, Marty poured daily doses of Catholic Mass into me to save my soul, the same as she did Senna Tea to keep me regular. Yet, by the time I witnessed the accident, meditation was the closest I came to praying any more.

The day the train killed Ismelda, people who had been drawn to the accident crossed themselves, recited the Rosary, and said Hail Marys out loud.

Sobbing more inward than out, I closed my eyes right there at the tracks and talked directly to God.

First I thanked him for not putting me on the same side of the tracks with Ismelda when she jumped and fell under the train. After having dug the bodies out of the storm drain a few weeks back, I think I would have lost my mind if I had been the agent chasing Ismelda when she, too, died.

Then I apologized for being glad I didn't cross the tracks behind Mr. Guzman because the train would have hit me and stopped, thus saving Ismelda's life. Being glad for me was a death wish for her. I thought, *I could be dead right now and forever.* The moment I internalized the finality of what death meant, I felt woozy. Death and dying was all around me and somehow I managed to live.

My thoughts switched between me not being dead to Ismelda and Shaun being dead for all time to Marty with death soon coming to get her. When I remembered the clammy coldness of death I'd felt on the bodies I dug out of the drain, I wondered if all dead bodies had that chilled latex feel about them. Then I thought of the people I knew who were dead. Shaun, José, Brinell, Sister Margaret, half the kids I knew growing up who had died of drug overdoses, AIDS, or were killed in street or gang violence; Mr. Rose, Billy Rose's father was dead, too. Now Ismelda.

They all died. Night fell. The sun rose the next morning. Winter came, then spring, summer, and fall. Each one died and nothing else changed.

Then it occurred to me, not one of those deaths had had any more effect on the earth's rotation than man landing on the moon. A chill shot down my spine and radiated out to every pore. I trembled uncontrollably even though the temperature outside was ninety-five degrees.

The purpose of death's coming and taking people away seemed to be only to make room for more people. It reminded me of something the minister used to say during communion at the community church I attended while in college. "As these retire, let others come."

Death retired people so others could come, making death and birth a revolving door, showing us that life goes on with or without us.

And what was I doing with my gift of life? I was looking for a drug smuggler named Mexican Joe. For what? To retire him so others could come?

If you'd been able to kill him, he'd already be dead.

The words came at me so loud and clear I opened my eyes to see who had said them, though I knew no one had.

No one had to tell me I was not a cold blooded killer, just as no one had to tell me my destiny did not lie in killing Mexican Joe. Besides, if I only killed him, he wouldn't feel a lifetime of suffering and misery like he inflicted upon many others and upon me. As a law enforcement officer, however, there were things I could do to make his life a living hell, but would not cause me to lose a moment of peace after having done them.

The train incident was the worst tragedy I had ever witnessed. It shook my inner resolve the way a small earthquake moves fine china, rearranging it on the shelf, but not breaking it. Poor Mr. Guzman. I saw the accident from under the train and didn't get the full impact he had witnessed from his perspective. He must have been devastated. I started toward him, to offer comfort.

He saw me approaching, turned, and walked away.

I remembered the concern in his eyes and his voice when he told me to stay away from Mexican Joe, concern of a caring man. He couldn't have witnessed the mutilation and death of Ismelda without feeling pain or discomfort, but he never mentioned those feelings to me.

I never mentioned to him that I heard him cry.

At times over the next few days, when Mr. Guzman and I looked into each other's eyes, something told me he struggled with memories scarring him even more than this one. Still I kept my distance, let him work it out in his own way.

As usual, I took strength in meditation. Then something Marty said made me remember she was much smarter than her actions sometimes implied.

"The train was only a machine," she said. "A machine speeding toward a destination unknown to it, through no choice of its own. Ismelda had a choice. She may not have chosen wisely, but the choice to jump for the train was her own."

I knew that, but knowing didn't stop me from having occasional nightmares.

CHAPTER TWENTY-FIVE

Billy Rose's father died five days after Shaun's death. To be absolutely accurate, I should say Billy Rose's mother killed him.

Mr. Rose had spent that Saturday afternoon drinking beer and cleaning his collection of guns, which ranged from an AK-47 to a Revolutionary War musket to the 12-gauge sawed off shotgun that took his life.

According to the police report, Mr. Rose had put all the guns away except the shotgun, which he had won in payment for a bet. He didn't have papers permitting him to legally own it, but it was his most prized acquisition.

Mrs. Rose had been playing waitress to her husband's incessant demands for food and drinks all afternoon. This last time she brought him a beer and accidentally spilled suds on the barrel of the shotgun.

Mr. Rose hit his wife, knocking her into the table he used to put his gun collection on while cleaning it, and on which the shotgun still lay.

Off balance and wobbly, Mrs. Rose put her hands out to steady herself and grabbed hold of the shotgun. She picked it up and blasted out his heart.

Despite the hour-and-a-half delay between the time the incident occurred and the time she reported it to them, the police never brought charges against Mrs. Rose.

Her explanation for the delay: "The kickback from the gun knocked me into the wall where I bumped my head, making me unconscious for a while. When I woke up, I was fuzzy and disoriented, so I called my friend, Marty, in Rio Rico. She told me to call the police right away and I thought I did but I must have passed out again. Well, now you know why I waited until Marty got here before making the call."

Marty said Mrs. Rose was nervous, stuttering, and alternately wringing her hands, wiping her eyes and nose, and drying them on her skirt as she gave her statement.

Although they had not actually been as close as Mrs. Rose's description seemed to imply, Marty faithfully stood by her during the police interrogation.

"She was still scared of him," Marty later said, when she told me the story. "The man was fuckin' dead and she was still scared of him. I guess she thought his ghost was going to fly up and bop her one in the mouth."

"You probably would have been scared, too," I said.

"The hell I would," she said. "The first time that man hit me is when I would've blown his ass away."

I believed her. As long as I'd known Marty, and as many men as I'd seen her with, I'd never seen but one raise his hand to hit her. When he did, she broke the longneck bottle she had been holding on the corner of the table and yelled, "Come on, sucker." He went the other way, out the front door, and he never came back.

Of course, I did see the psychological and physical abuse Mrs. Rose endured.

And the police had documented reports of abuse dating back to a week after the Rose family moved to Tucson when Billy Rose and I were kids. That first time it was Marty who called them and said, "The man next door is beating the crap outta his wife."

Mr. Rose had never been charged with spousal abuse, however, because Mrs. Rose was always too afraid to testify. She would lie and swear she walked into a doorknob, or fell down the steps, or slipped in the bathtub. If those things had been true all those times, she would have been in *The Guinness Book of World Records* for being the most accident-prone woman alive.

Mr. Rose's brother maintained that Mr. Rose would never clean his guns while they were loaded.

Although he hadn't been talking to her, Marty quickly replied, "A drunk don't always know what he's doing." She added, "Being one, I got some personal knowledge of their strange behavior."

The police must have accepted Mrs. Rose's account of the incident because they closed the case less than a month after it occurred.

I was preparing for Shaun's funeral when Mr. Rose was killed. Having been a victim of his violence, I was among the group that did not cry at his passing. I never said so, but I secretly relished the fact that before he was shot, he knew it was going to happen, just as I had known all those years ago what he was going to do to me.

Billy Rose disappeared after Shaun's death and was still missing when his father was killed and buried. When he returned, I met him at the airport and explained what had happened.

He was shocked more by his mother's actions than anything.

About his mother, he said, "Who'd have thought she'd eventually stand up to him after taking his shit and protecting him all those years?"

About his father, he said, "It couldn't have happened to a more deserving guy."

To this day, Billy Rose has never visited the gravesite on which Mrs. Rose dutifully places fresh flowers each month.

HASTA MAÑANA

Go figure. She said she still loved the man he was when she first met him, and except for what he did when he lost his temper, he took good care of her.

I said Mrs. Rose's grieving posture was for the police. There's no statute of limitation on murder, and the police can be devious when they're trying to make a case. They know that, just as a drunk acts differently when he's drinking, the family of a drunk acts differently when he's drinking, too. Sometimes they aid and abet. Sometimes they lie and cry. And sometimes they patiently wait until an opportunity presents itself so perfectly that it looks like destiny put it there; they seize the moment, then sort out the details later.

My secret theory was that Mrs. Rose had a secret, too. And she believed if she appeared too happy her husband was dead, the police might change their minds and decide to charge her with something.

Later I discovered Mrs. Rose did have a secret. It just wasn't what I thought.

Billy Rose knew why I did not grieve Mr. Rose's passing. He knew I understood his sentiments about his father "getting what he deserved." And he also knew I wasn't offended when he said, "Funny, but blasting the bastard to smithereens seems more *your* mother's style than mine."

It was true. Mrs. Rose was passive by nature and Marty was aggressive. It took me years to understand; even when Marty chose to be passive, it was her method of getting her way and ultimately controlling the situation, which is, after all, the goal of aggression.

I remembered Billy Rose's statement about personal styles several times over the first few days following the train accident in regard to Mr. Guzman, who no longer acted in the style I had come to know during our first rotation. This rotation he was by the book, by the clock, and hardly ever without a phone in his hand when we weren't in active pursuit of illegals. I didn't know at the time who he was talking to, but it wasn't the dispatcher back at the facility, because he used his personal cell phone to make the calls and sometimes he would turn his back to me as if he thought I could read his lips.

Other times Mr. Guzman looked over at me when he was making these calls and his eyes searched mine. At first I thought he was looking for some specific knowledge that would have been reflected in my eyes if I had it, and not if I didn't. Later I came to understand he knew something and couldn't decide whether or not it was time for me to know it, too.

During low times, when Mr. Guzman would not talk to me, I had plenty of time to reflect and I often went back to my "prayer session" the day of the train accident. The more I replayed it in my mind, the clearer it became to me that the only mandate I had to hunt down Mexican Joe was the one I had put on myself. The more I accepted that as truth, the more I knew an unconscious decision not to kill Mexican Joe had been made the day I talked to God.

After that, my life took on a brand new meaning. I began to awaken each morning without thinking, *This might be the day I kill Mexican Joe.* And that was good. Even if no one had seen me kill him, or ever figured out I was the one who had done it, I would have carried the guilt in my mind forever. I would have never known another moment's peace. Mexican Joe would have won yet another victory.

As this was being internalized, I wanted to talk to Mr. Guzman, to tell him my newfound revelation, to let him know the change I was having in my heart and in my plan. He was the only one, other than Billy Rose and Marty, who

HASTA MAÑANA

knew anything about Mexican Joe, but the few times I started to say something to him not concerned with work, he stopped me cold. Other times he kept his distance, making personal communication between us impossible. In fact, for the remainder of the two-week rotation, I talked to him more on the radio than I did face to face.

Because Mr. Guzman was so standoffish and cold, I was glad to see Billy Rose when he returned from the East Coast. I welcomed his concern and caring and I especially relished the opportunity to talk to someone interested in listening to what I had to say. Marty now had Miguel to talk to and I had no other friends in the area. I hadn't looked up the kids I had known as a child when I moved back from California; my erratic work schedule and long hours didn't lend to making new friendships.

Billy Rose and I were getting on so well I decided to go to Guadalajara with him. As the time we were to leave approached, I anxiously looked forward to the trip. I had been into several border towns, but other than Puerto Penasco, two hundred and twenty-six miles from Nogales, I'd never been into the Mexican interior.

I studied maps and looked up historical sites and jotted down everything I wanted to do. Granted, I wouldn't do most of it this trip. Billy Rose was driving Shaun's red truck to Guadalajara rather than us flying. Of course, it wasn't advisable for tourists to travel that far into the Mexican interior in a private car, but Billy Rose had done it so many times over the past few years without incident, he felt safe doing it again. So, I highlighted all the historical landmarks that I wanted to see along the way. He promised to stop at the ones on our travel route.

I had always been a history buff and for reasons unknown to me my interest had intensified since moving back to Arizona. Could it have been because the earth, the mountains, the relics here spoke of the Old Ones? I swear there are times when I am alone that they communicate with me. Not in words, but in ways I understood.

Could my intensified interest in the history of the southwest have been because the juxtaposition of distinct cultures never lets me forget it had been Mexican land much longer than it had been American?

Or, could it simply have been that delving into the past was a way of looking for a light to the future, my way of keeping the emotional rudder of my soul steering true?

I didn't know the underlying reason, and I didn't think this five-day trip would be any more than a chance to relax and maybe soak up a little of my ancestors' culture.

I couldn't have been more wrong.

CHAPTER TWENTY-SIX

"There's good and bad in everybody," Marty always told me, usually in defense of herself.

Long ago I came to understand her bits of wisdom weren't automatically false just because she said them. I was now beginning to accept without disdain that many things she said were grounded in truth and evidenced an uncanny understanding of human nature and the order of things.

Take Sale Day in Nogales, for instance. I had done good and bad. The good was apprehending a hoard of people trying to illegally enter the U.S. Some would not agree with me, but getting Jorge's money for him was also a good thing.

The bad thing I did on Sale Day was to let my search for Mexican Joe come between my job and me. Conversely, by some glitch in the universal theorem of cause and effect, seeing him probably stopped me from jumping the train tracks a few seconds behind Mr. Guzman, thus preventing me from becoming one with the railroad ties.

So Marty opined, "You got Mexican Joe to thank for saving your life."

Although I accept much of Marty's wisdom, her natural order of things and mine have not completely melded. But if I did take her deduction as truth, and Mexican Joe did in fact save my life, then her cultural-based logic would reasonably conclude that he saved my life so I can one day save his.

That's a cosmic kick in the ass if ever there was one.

But it worked out for the best. After that day, when I meditated I could acknowledge on a rational and unemotional level that Mexican Joe did not force Shaun to take the drugs, which killed him. Shaun had had a choice and he made the wrong one, just as Ismelda did.

In my life I've made right and wrong choices many times, too. For example, I did what was right for Shaun when I stopped fooling around with alcohol and drugs in the early stages of my pregnancy. But I did wrong when I gave Shaun to the Roses the day he was born. I realized my mistake and wanted to rectify it, but Shaun was taken away from me. And after his death, I wanted to prove I loved Shaun by exacting revenge on Mexican Joe, the person Billy Rose had fingered as being responsible.

But none of that would change the irrefutable fact. Shaun was dead.

Shaun is dead.

Shaun will always be dead.

Life goes on.

It was hard for me to objectively look into my heart and lay my motives out for introspection. But after Miguel and his family in the drain, after Ismelda, after accepting the inevitability of Marty's terminal illness, I could no longer justify feeling sorry for myself the way I had before I became a Border Patrol Agent. My acceptance of life going on with or without me was tantamount to my saying I wanted to go on and be a part of it as long as I could. To be able to go on with my life, I couldn't wake up each day hiding from who I was and what I'd done. To be able to do that, I couldn't kill Mexican Joe in cold blood.

Cause and effect right down the line.

I hadn't figured out all the dynamics of the psychological

HASTA MAÑANA

transformation taking place in my head, but between the time Ismelda jumped for the train, and Billy Rose and I left for Guadalajara, I was no longer looking for Mexican Joe.

But my life had already intersected with his. When I stopped looking for Mexican Joe, he came looking for me.

CHAPTER TWENTY-SEVEN

"I'm not going to kill him," I told Billy Rose. "But the gusto in Mexican Joe's living is about to go flat. As soon as we get back from Guadalajara, you're going to use your genius and put him into our computers . . ."

He interrupted. "Thanks for asking."

I ignored his attitude. "With seven thousand Border Patrol Agents carrying his picture around he should have a hard time taking a leak, let alone crossing the border."

He looked up at me and said, "Unless he's a U.S. citizen."

"What are you trying to say?" It had not occurred to me Mexican Joe was anything but Mexican.

Billy Rose didn't answer. He was unpacking everything I had previously packed for our trip. Then he repacked it his way.

We both wore khaki shorts, yellow silk tees, and khaki canvas shoes, which he said were good for the traveling we were doing. Billy Rose was the consummate traveler of our duo and he averaged two to three weeks a month on the road, which was the reason our living arrangement worked as well as it did. He was home long enough to pay the bills, clean his clothes, and get on my nerves. Then he left.

"What's that supposed to mean, Billy Rose?" My tone was a little more insistent and a lot more strident than I had intended. "Do you know something I don't?"

"Jesus, Miriam." His tone expressed his exasperation with the subject. "Can't you give it a rest until we get back?

We'll talk about putting him into the computer then."

"Promise?"

"I promise."

He looked at me now. He would deny it till his face turned as blue as his eyes, but inside he was laughing at me when he said, "And your speech about not killing Mexican Joe. I wouldn't have told you about him in the first place if I thought you could. You don't have the killer instinct."

I flinched.

He smiled.

"It's okay," he said. "That's a good thing. If you were a killer you'd have gotten rid of the baby when you first got pregnant. It was legal and you still couldn't do it." He looked very serious, then. "But you have to admit, if you had done it then, none of this other stuff would've happened now."

He finished packing my bag, closed and locked it, then put it by the door next to his, which was identical in color and size.

With his back to me, Billy Rose couldn't see the look on my face. He knew it still upset me to talk about Shaun's beginning and end in a casual manner. Yet it seemed to me he interjected it into the conversation whenever possible. Now he was putting a sick twist on "kill him now or kill him later" by implying Shaun's death was my fault because I didn't kill him before he was born.

Billy Rose was right about the pregnancy, though. He had urged me to terminate it. Even Marty, good Catholic that she was, said she couldn't go with me to do it, but she would give her permission, if needed, to have it done.

"I wasn't much older than you when I got pregnant," Marty had said. "I've never been sorry a day since I had you. But," she reluctantly added, "I'd be lying if I said I never wondered what my life would have been if I hadn't."

Marty had avoided my eyes, perhaps so I couldn't see into her heart. "Everybody can tell you about having a baby," she said. "But nothing they tell you will ever prepare you for the sacrifices you have to make to raise a child. You've got to be willing to give all your energy, your resources, even your life, for your child. And God forgive me, Miriam, I was never able to make that complete a sacrifice." She sniffed back the tears from her eyes. "My life came first, most times, and I know you suffered because of it."

It's true I had suffered some. But after the day she said that to me, whenever I considered the alternative, I stopped complaining. So I had Shaun, then I gave him away. And now I know what my life was like without him in it. What I'm left with is the unanswerable question of what my life would have been like if I had raised Shaun myself.

Billy Rose always told me his constant reference to Shaun was for my benefit. "You need a reality infusion," he said. "You keep things inside. What with meditating and all, you never tell me what's on your mind anymore. I mean, not the important stuff like you used to. What you need to do is get over it and get on with your life. You know, turn the page."

I reminded myself this philosophical wellspring was flowing from a thirty-two-year-old man still trapped in the body of a teenage boy who couldn't get past his first love. And who still liked us to dress alike, to tag me as being with him.

But I didn't speak to his needs. Since he was talking about mine, I expanded on that topic.

"What I need, Billy Rose, is for you to stop telling me what I need," I told him the first time he infused me with reality. "Shaun was my son. I'll get over him when I'm good and ready and not one second before."

"It's for your own good."

"That's not for you to decide." Then I changed the subject.

Today when Billy Rose tried his armchair guru pep talk, I didn't respond at all. I went to the bedroom window, slanted the blinds against the strong rays of the early morning sun, and began to edit the information I'd concocted to put on Mexican Joe's file when we came back. I knew the truth of it all. And the truth was that Billy Rose was right when he said I didn't have a killer instinct. He was wrong, though, to mistake it as an inability to respond as though I did.

In retrospect, I probably should have taken the time to explain to Billy Rose that I'm enough like Marty to sacrifice someone else's life, if it comes down to theirs or mine.

But at the time I didn't realize it was something he would ever need to know.

CHAPTER TWENTY-EIGHT

Early that Thursday morning in August, Billy Rose and I set out for Guadalajara in Shaun's red truck. I still referred to it as Shaun's truck, but it had never been his truck at all.

It had always been Billy Rose's truck.

"Either I'm too old for this truck, or this truck is too juvenile for me," he had said one morning. He later came home with a BMW roadster, the model from the James Bond movie. He was going to give the truck to Shaun for his sixteenth birthday. A nice, big brotherly thing to do, only Shaun never lived to be sixteen.

The Roses had planned a big bash for Shaun's birthday, which would fall on Saturday. Father Angelo, our family priest, was going to be with me when I had my private talk with Shaun, after the other partygoers had left. I had cleared this with Mr. Rose and he agreed. I could tell Shaun I was his mother and Billy Rose was his father.

That was enough to satisfy me, but it never happened.

Shaun and his two best friends went out that Friday night to celebrate their last night of bumming rides. Billy Rose dropped them off at the mall where all the kids hung out on the weekend. And then Shaun was dead.

Shaun's friends would not snitch where they got the drugs. Now they never will. Three months after Shaun's death, the police announced they were close to making an arrest, but then they lost their witnesses. The bodies of the two boys were found together. Both had been shot in the head, execution style.

On the morning we left for Guadalajara, the air was clear of smoke from the still burning rainforest fires. The cloudless sky was bright and open. I was hopeful.

Billy Rose took I-19 south from our apartment in Green Valley to the port in Nogales. Since we would drive a personal vehicle into Mexico, he had secured an import permit for the truck and Mexican automobile insurance for the length of stay. I would fly back in four days. He would stay for a week or more.

A few years back, when his travel escalated, Billy Rose had bought identical body pouches for us to carry passports, drivers' licenses, visas, traveler's checks, and emergency information, like the number to the American Embassy in each of the countries he customarily entered. The pouches were soft kid-glove leather, had a waterproof lining, and a two-inch wide band so they could be comfortably strapped to the body beneath clothing. We wore them today.

Since unleaded gas can be scarce in less populated areas in Mexico, some of which we would drive through, Billy Rose carried extra with us.

"I don't want those things in this truck," I'd said when he put the containers behind our seats. "The fumes are nauseous and they might explode."

"Don't be stupid. The gas tank on the truck doesn't explode, does it?"

"Speaking of which, the truck has an extra tank to carry gas for emergencies."

"Have you ever driven in Mexico?"

He asked the question to make a point because he already knew the answer was, "No."

"Well, I have. In Mexico, the gas situation is like it was here in the states when we had to ration gas, odd-even days. You can't chance getting stranded on the road, because the only people who will stop to help you are the ones who will rob you. You can't even trust the police not to be banditos. Is that what you want to be up against? If so," he pointed to the gas can, "we can leave it here."

He then grabbed the handle of the gas can as though he was going to heft it out of the truck on my say-so. It was obvious he enjoyed every worst-case scenario thought running through my mind while I deliberated answers.

Asshole.

"Okay," I acquiesced. "Leave the damn thing where it is, but if it explodes, don't say I didn't warn you."

He looked at me until he realized I knew the absurdity of what I'd just said. "Get in the truck, Miriam. Sometimes I think you say dumb shit just to get me going, so I'll forget what we were talking about."

It usually worked, too.

We cleared Mexican customs and headed south on I-15, down the eastern side of the Gulf of California, through Hermosilla to Guaymas, where we stopped at a local restaurant overlooking the coast. We only ate what had been overcooked, bought oranges that could be peeled for dessert, and waited until we returned to the truck to drink bottled water from home.

We gassed up, used the facilities, and were back on the road within the hour. We rushed because we wanted to get to Mazatlãn, where we would spend the night, and it was three hundred miles away. On Friday we would drive to Culiacán, in the state of Sinoloa, then drive down the coast to Puerta Vallarta and stay the night. On Saturday we would drive inland a hundred fifty miles to Guadalajara.

HASTA MAÑANA

Sunday we would act like tourists and on Monday morning I would fly home.

Billy Rose would drive home, returning two days later. That was the plan.

CHAPTER TWENTY-NINE

Present-day Mexico is a blend of medieval Spanish religion and Native American culture, sprinkled here and there with Italian and African customs. But the heart and soul of Mexico are the ancient Aztec and Mayan civilizations upon which it was founded.

The resort areas of Mexico are Americanized, some have ultra-exotic conveniences, and the language you barter for authentic souvenirs in is English. But driving away from the tourist areas, the rutted, unpaved roads look like mini earthquakes ripped the earth apart. I was disheartened to see garbage discarded along the roadside like a tandem sewer. Many homes were nothing more than shacks topped by corrugated tin roofs with window openings but no sashes.

However, it wasn't until the morning we drove into Culiacán and I was immersed in local color, that I became fearful.

Billy Rose said I moaned and groaned everywhere we had stopped along the way. My complaint: "This is like being in Nogales or El Paso or East L.A."

"You wanna see local culture?" Billy Rose said when we got to Culiacán. "I'll show you local culture."

Every thing I knew about Culiacán I learned at work. That should be a clue to the content of my information. I knew it as the capital of the Mexican State of Sinoloa, a drug-rich coastal city of six hundred thousand. Agents were told most migrants and cocaine headed for the U.S. pass through Culiacán. So, when I looked out of the window of our truck at the many men talking on cell phones, I didn't think they were calling home to see if they needed to bring milk and bread.

Thinking I'd probably caught some of the same men crossing the border and they would recognize me, a dollop of fear greased my stomach the entire time we were in Culiacán. I'd swear I saw more guns carried by men in civilian clothes than I'd seen on police officers in uniform back home. And most disconcerting, all my expertise with weapons meant nothing here. Here I couldn't carry a gun. Until that moment, I hadn't realized how comforting it was to have my weapon close at hand.

Billy Rose took delight in telling me, "If we arrived here via public transportation, we would have to get off the bus or train, then go through a metal detector before we could enter the station."

"You've convinced me," I said. "Let's go."

He laughed and said, "Not yet. And if you're thinking about getting out to walk, remember the *muchachos* will rob you blind; the big boys will do even worse."

After a few more blocks, he didn't have to tell me the smell of stale urine, frying tortillas, and brewing salsa comingled to make a fragrance that couldn't be bottled and sold. Even closing the windows didn't help.

The men, eyeing our red truck possessively from the streets, wore tattoos and baseball caps set backwards on their heads. The men who revved their engines to challenge us to race them, drove Dodge Rams and Chevy pick-ups with oversized wheels and jacked up suspensions, causing them to tower over our truck, which had been lowered and sported small wheels. Their trucks had fins or railings and silver hood ornaments shaped like bulls or horses. Our hood was bare except for bugs splattered on it during the drive.

"Where are we going?" I demanded.

"To the Governor's Palace," was all Billy Rose would say.

When he did stop, it was in front of a strange-looking building.

"Is this some kind of joke?" I asked.

"I assure you it's no joke," Billy Rose laughed. "This is a very popular shrine dedicated to Jesus Malverde, a criminal hanged in 1909. He's now known as *El Narcosanton.*"

Of course, I'd heard of *El Narcosanton* many times and was astonished to see the shrine was built of plate glass, white bathroom tile, and corrugated sheet metal.

"You should see the inside," he said. "The statue is plastic and surrounded by candles."

"You mean you actually went in there?"

"Of course. You wanna go in?"

"Hell, no."

"Why not?"

"Have you looked around us?" I couldn't believe myself what I saw. "Those men are flaunting their guns like 1920s hoodlums."

Billy Rose laughed again. "They don't call this 'little Chicago' for nothing. Besides, they wouldn't consider themselves hoodlums. They're drug lords. *El Narcosanton* is the Big Narco Saint and they come here to pray for good fortune."

"If that's why they come, Billy Rose, why are we here?"

"I have to meet a client in the Governor's Palace," he said and pointed to a huge ceramic and stone structure situated on well-manicured grounds, about a football field away. "Since you wanted to soak up some local culture," he smiled, "I thought we'd stop here first."

HASTA MAÑANA

"I didn't mean fucking drug lords, Billy Rose. I see enough of them on my job."

"No," he said, shaking his head in a way that implied I was pathetically ill informed. "You don't see drug lords on your job. The people you see back home are expendable peons. Most of them don't get as close to a drug lord as you are now. The drug lords are like the CEOs of big companies. Saying you see them at the border smuggling drugs is like saying you see Fahed behind the perfume counter of Harrods selling fragrances. The narcotics business is a multibillion-dollar organization, Miriam. Practically everybody here helps to grow, sell, buy, and smuggle drugs, or knows somebody who does and keeps their mouth shut. But as long as you don't bother them, they won't bother you."

"Let's go." I turned in my seat to glare at him.

"Why?" He smiled and cocked his head to one side. "You da' man, remember? The highly trained federal agent who pulled a gun on me in my own damned apartment. Do you know how that made me feel?" He didn't wait for an answer. "I'll tell you how. Like *pinche caca*."

"Okay, Billy Rose. I understand you felt like shit, but can't we talk about this after we leave here?"

"Sure," he smiled. "As soon as you tell me what you're afraid of."

"Right now I'm afraid of you," I admitted. "You're acting like you're crazy. But I know what this is all about. This is about you showing me how tough you are and what a pussy I am, and not the other way around, like it really is.

"Well, you've made your point. Even with all my training, I'm scared. But scaring me doesn't mean you're brave," I said. "In fact, all it does is make you some kind of a creep who's holding me here against my will.

"Ever since I've known you, Billy Rose, you've been a

revenge freak, but this is a new low even for you."

His expression didn't change. "You still haven't told me what you're afraid of. Everywhere you look you see men with guns, either the police, banditos, or guards. That's a fact of life when you travel away from the resorts in this country.

"If you're afraid, with all your expert training, how do you think the average Jane Doe who lives here feels? Add to that the living conditions and the economy, and it's no wonder three out of four of them outsmart you guys at the border and cross without getting caught."

As far as I was concerned, Billy Rose had dug a six-foot hole when he took me to this place. He stepped in the hole when he gave his pro-drug spiel. Every minute he kept me there belittling the Border Patrol, he backfilled the hole around him until all I could see was a curly mop top on an indistinguishable face without personality or character.

When we left the shrine and started for the Governor's Palace, I sat in the corner of my seat, wedged against the door, looking into my side mirror. If I hadn't been sulking, I wouldn't have seen the black Lincoln Navigator with a tombstone on its plates. My first thought was, *Tourist from Arizona.* But the vehicle stayed behind us when we turned the first corner and the next; my instincts told me it was more than a mere coincidence. I couldn't see the driver through his darkened windshield, but the big black Navigator looked sinister. I shivered.

"We're being followed," I whispered to Billy Rose.

"Why do you think that?" He looked in the rearview mirror.

"I know that SUV," Billy Rose said. "He wouldn't hurt you." He turned into an empty parking space in front of the Governor's Palace and stopped the truck.

HASTA MAÑANA

The black Navigator continued to the end of the block and turned right.

Not one person had tried to harm us since arriving in Culiacán, and Billy Rose reminded me of that over and over again. Still, I didn't appreciate his method of infusing reality and my anger ran hot. Billy Rose hadn't told me who was in the SUV, so when we checked into a hotel my attitude toward him had not softened. In fact, under these circumstances, I wasn't sure I was going to continue the trip. My actual thought was, *If I catch a flight home in the morning, I can use the rest of my days off moving and be out of the apartment before Billy Rose returns.*

"I will never forget what you did to me today," I told him. "And I will never forgive you, either."

"You've never forgiven anybody for anything since you got raped when you were thirteen years old. I know you thought today was a little over the top, but I swear to God, you were never in any danger." He turned to go to the bathroom, and then turned back, almost as an afterthought. "You know, you've always been a bit too melodramatic for my taste."

Billy Rose slept like a baby that night.

I didn't sleep at all.

CHAPTER THIRTY

When Billy Rose sleeps, moist curls form blond ringlets, which catch on his ears and plaster his forehead. Off and on a smile plays at the corner of his cupid bow lips and he looks so vulnerable I want to take him in my arms and protect him from the world. Marty thinks the world should be protected from Billy Rose.

Once when we were young, he fell asleep on our couch. Marty saw the smile and said, "He's dreaming of devilment, but disguises it by looking like an angel."

Marty never liked Billy Rose. "He scares me," she said when I brought him home from school the first time. "His aura is cracked."

"But that's the same thing you said about me," I reminded her.

"I did," she said. "But you live in the same world as the rest of us. He lives in his head."

We'd had enough of these talks for me to follow her thinking; still he was the brand new friend I'd successfully defended against the playground bully and I moved easily into defending him from her.

"How do you know where he lives?" I asked. "Can you see inside his head?"

"No," she admitted, but not with an angry voice. "Looking in his eyes I can see his mind working as fast as one of those calculating machines. You hear it making a noise, but can't see what it's doing."

"Since you can read his mind," I said, "tell me what he's thinking."

"I can see it working," she answered. "I didn't say I could read it like a book. Probably be one those Freddy Krueger horror stories, though."

Billy Rose and I aged, and I understood what Marty had meant. Being his constant companion, I learned to second-guess him most times, yet there were moments when he went so deep into his soul even I couldn't follow. He had gone there yesterday when he was taunting me.

As he slept this morning, the old Billy Rose seemed to be back, making it hard for me to believe he had been such a jerk when we arrived in Culiacán. Still, knowing he'd scared me into near cardiac arrest because I'd mistakenly pulled a gun on him weeks before, left me with a lingering disquietude. I'd done worse to him than that.

Billy Rose was big on revenge.

What would he do to me when he found out Shaun was not his son?

When he was in high school, Billy Rose wrote a paper advocating the legalization of marijuana. It was in the early 1980s and he was in a gifted and talented class. His mentor, a tall, lithe, Princeton graduate student with blue eyes and black hair, had gifts and talents of her own. She was also a Volunteer in Service to America Teacher who came from a wealthy family, which had gotten its money through hard work. It seems her grandfather stipulated she work among the common people for three years, hoping to humble her before she received the mountain of money affectionately known as her trust fund.

Under her tutelage, Billy Rose's paper was well written and well researched. It quoted extensively from the writings of Timothy Leary and won Billy Rose first prize in the school district writing contest. Naturally the news media published the essay and the school board had it delivered to them over breakfast the next morning. The average age of the school board was forty-eight and it still had more starch in it than a Van Heusen shirt. Collectively it was not amused.

When the school board was not amused, it went into immediate action, and reaction kicked in with a domino effect. The last one to fall booted Billy Rose out of school; after he refused to pen an equally well written but better researched, discredit Timothy Leary, anti-legalization of marijuana paper. While he waited for his ACLU lawyer to get him reinstated, Billy Rose bought a nickel bag of marijuana and put it in the gym locker of the principal's son.

Billy Rose reported the story to me via phone, Tucson to San Diego. Since his subterfuge would have no dire consequences if no one knew the drugs were in the locker, he tipped the police who raided the locker and arrested the boy.

But that wasn't good enough for Billy Rose.

To insure the principal knew he was the one responsible, Billy Rose told a few kids known for their snitching tendencies what he had done. The principal went to the Rose's house and choked Billy Rose until he turned blue. In the end the school board had no choice but to fire the principal. What else could they do?

After Billy Rose recuperated, he returned to school with an official apology from the school board, and without having to rewrite the paper.

Then revenge was sweet enough for Billy Rose.

The irony in the story is that Billy Rose has never used illegal drugs. "If the only choice is between giving drugs to my mother and taking them myself," he once said, "she'll be stoned."

"The person who sells you drugs controls you," he'd preach to us kids. He was only a kid himself, but he understood the power of control. His father had so tightly controlled him, he came to resist constraints in any form. He even wore boxer shorts.

But his disdain for control never stopped him from trying to control others.

I never consciously wanted to control Billy Rose. For most of our adult relationship, I'd just as soon he left me alone, but he was as annoying as a fly swarming too close to my face. I'd swat him away and he'd bounce right back like a tethered ball. Lately, I'd come to understand my detachment was a part of my appeal to him. His need to control me bound him to me with doglike devotion, then he could fetch and carry and amuse me and make me laugh. In these small ways he sometimes prompted my mood, but he took every small victory as part of the whole that he wanted to achieve.

Two cracked auras, Marty had said. Billy Rose's and mine. "One cracked from knocking against boundaries. One cracked from being beaten down."

I started meditating, using reason and reconciliation, hoping someday my aura would mend.

Billy Rose did not believe in auras. He continued to plot intricate ruses for revenge and I know more than once he exacted retribution.

CHAPTER THIRTY-ONE

Come sunrise, I was still sitting in the brocade-covered wing chair by the window, my knees drawn up to my chin and strapped together by my arms to make a pillow for my head. I hadn't slept though; hadn't even undressed. Yet I wasn't nearly as angry as I had been the night before. As the red haze faded from the sky and morning began to brighten, my thoughts turned to how I could help Billy Rose save face. How we could reweave the hole he'd ripped in the seam of trust that had for so many years held us unquestioningly together. My anger had eased enough to still want to try and be a friend.

I stood, stretched, slipped my feet back into my shoes, and went to the king-size bed he alone had used. I leaned down to stare at his face. Just the look of it brought back so many remembrances of times when he had been the sole pillar of my support system. Then shame rushed though me, fast and hot. How could I have doubted him? He wanted me to feel my mortality as he had felt his when I sighted him down the barrel of my gun; he only intended to scare me, not kill me.

I really was grateful for all the creature comforts he provided to make my existence comfortable and trouble free, though I had never asked for any of it, and could have managed on my own. My heart swelled with tenderness for the overgrown man-child who needed love and thought mine was for sale. I knew his ways as well as I knew my own. I should have expected him to retaliate; even the faithful dog sometimes turns. And a part of me truly did expect it. Billy Rose was known for carrying a grudge, pretending it wasn't even there. I expected he would let it simmer, but not ripen on this trip.

And, I had not expected him to be so harsh with me.

I reached my hand out, intending to smooth an errant curl.

He grabbed my wrist.

I screamed.

He held tight to my wrist. "What the hell do you think you're doing, Miriam?"

The tenderness, which had seconds before swelled my heart, vanished as if by magic. Anger rushed back in.

The worst was not yet over between us.

If his grip on my arm was any indication, it might never be over between us in a way that left the friendship intact.

He was hurting me. I wouldn't abide friend or foe that took such liberties.

"Did you hear me?" he yelled.

He knew I'd heard him. The people in the room two doors down probably heard him.

He jerked my wrist, pulling me close to him.

"What's your damned problem?" I hissed.

While it was true he'd caught me by surprise, he couldn't manhandle me. I was stronger than he was. I broke his finger-hold with my free hand, stood straight, and stepped back from the bed.

"You're my fucking problem," he snarled up at me from the bed. "Every problem I have starts, ends, or is intensified by you."

I rubbed my wrist. He was yelling at me, causing my already raw nerves to vibrate.

"Stop yelling at me, Billy Rose," I said. "I'm not your mother."

That one little innocuous sentence, which is probably uttered somewhere in the world every minute of every hour of every day, opened the valve to unleash Billy Rose's secret reservoir of anger.

He jumped from the bed and stood in one fluid motion. "Is that so?" He didn't try to cover his nakedness. "If you're not my mother, Miriam, then tell me why the hell you made a baby with my father?"

Whatever I had expected him to say it hadn't been that.

"How? What?" I stammered, locked eyes with him, and tried to voice my questions through staring.

He knew what I wanted to know.

"You didn't think I'd find out, did you?"

My voice left me. I could think of things to say, I didn't have speech to say them.

"All those years you let me think I was man enough to father a child, and guess what? I just ain't got the juice."

"How? What?" continued to be my level of articulation.

I was going to tell Billy Rose. One day. I swear I was. But only when I thought he could handle the truth without killing his father. He hated his father as a child and it got worse as he aged, so the day to tell him just never came. First Shaun was dead, then his father was dead, and then it didn't seem important anymore.

"How did I find out? You want to know how I found out? Someone in my Mensa group suggested I donate to the genius sperm bank, only they declined my application, referred me for further medical testing. Here I am thinking I have AIDS or something and the doctor tells me my count is too low to make a baby."

" 'But that can't be,' I told them.

" 'It can be and it is,' the doctor assured me. 'If some

girl's got you on the hook for child support, you're officially off.'

"Well, when I understood the science, the math wasn't hard to do," Billy Rose said. "Shaun looked so much like me, we had to be blood related. If I was shooting blanks, somebody else had to have a loaded pistol. One day when he was drunk, I asked my father why Shaun looked so much like me when I couldn't have children.

"He laughed in my face. Said there was a 'logical reason, Mr. Genius.' Said, 'Shaun is your half brother, that's why he looks like you.'

"Then the son of a bitch laughed until he nearly choked on his own spit. He bragged about 'his boy, the star athlete' and how Shaun was more of a man at fifteen than I'd ever be in my whole life."

That conversation must have taken place a few months before Shaun died, but reliving it had a visible effect on Billy Rose. His body twitched. His face contorted. A tear rolled down his cheek.

He brought his hand up and dried his eyes, rubbed the wetness between his fingers, brought them to his mouth, and licked the salty residue. His gaze met mine. I was so transfixed by the hate in his eyes I didn't see his hand moving until he slapped me hard across the face. Blood and mucous smeared the hand I slid across my mouth.

I felt what Mrs. Rose must have felt the day she killed Mr. Rose. I may have done the same if I had had my gun.

"Why did you let me believe he was my baby?" The spit from his screech sprayed my face.

I quickly reverted to my meditation mode, the only way I could absorb the pain without crying out. Then with all the calmness and focus I had learned to harness from chaos, I picked up the laptop and threw it dead center of his head.

All the while I was doing this, I was thinking, Billy Rose knew for a fact his father had raped me. He came back from the supermarket with his mother and found the man on top of me, grunting like a pig, me clawing and scratching, trying to fight him off. He knocked his father off me with a frozen log of Park's sausage from the supermarket bag he'd just brought inside with him.

The thought should have crossed his mind, and the mind of Mrs. Rose, who stood post-still watching, mouth open, saying nothing.

When Mr. Rose was knocked off me, I screamed obscenities while I got my clothes on. Then I scrambled to my feet and lunged for the cutlery drawer intending to get the butcher knife, but Billy Rose got there first and held it closed. It was the only time in our relationship he got the best of me.

Mr. Rose was only slightly dazed from being hit on the head. He grabbed his wallet, threw all the money in it on the floor, and said, "Tell your fucking Ma the next time she sells me something, it'd better come with a warranty."

What had he meant by that? I was hurt and humiliated, now his words confused me. What did my mother have to do with what had just happened?

"I'm going to get Marty." I started for the back door. "She'll call the police. We'll be back."

Billy Rose scooped up the money and jumped in front of the door. "Take the money." He reached it toward me.

I jumped back, I didn't know why, but taking money for what had just been done to me didn't seem right.

Billy Rose could see how I felt. "Just think about this, Miriam," he said, trying to calm me down. "It's over now. We can't go back and wish it away.

"Why shouldn't you keep the money? You earned it. We

could use it to go to the Sting concert this weekend."

I should have realized he was thinking ahead, not about the moment. I did know he'd been conniving for two weeks to get money for the concert, but right then I wanted him to think about me first. All he could think of was "free money," while I suffered dearly from the price I'd paid.

He insisted, "I hurt him more than he hurt you. I mean it's not like it was your first time or anything."

"Besides," he quickly added, "you can't tell the cops. You heard what he said. He paid your mother for the privilege."

I looked to Mrs. Rose for guidance. She abruptly turned and walked to the freezer, took out a cold compress, then headed toward Mr. Rose.

In the end I never told the police. I never said anything to Marty, either. I couldn't believe she would sell me to Mr. Rose. On the off-chance she had, I didn't ever want to know.

Three months later, when I started having morning sickness, we thought it was Billy Rose's baby. Then when I was six months pregnant, the doctor told me I was really seven. I reasoned that I would tell Billy Rose the baby came early then give it to the Roses to rear, as we had already planned to do. I would go to San Diego, as arranged by Father Angelo, and start a brand new life. That would solve all the problems.

But I didn't reason far enough to see Billy Rose following me to California as soon as he graduated high school. Nor did I have reason to believe my brand new life would have the same old people in it.

All this flashed through my mind in the instant it took me to pick up the laptop in the hotel room in Culiacán and hurl it through the air at Billy Rose's head.

He raised his arms before the laptop hit him, deflected it to the bed.

"Miriam, I'm sorry," he said, as though he'd relived the whole scene with me. He sounded different now. "Please. I'll never say anything like that again. I know what he did to you. I know you didn't tell me about the baby to protect me. I would have killed him and been locked away. See. That's why we belong together. You know what's best for me. Can't you see why I need you? I promise I'll never hit you again."

"You sure as hell won't." Flushing his plea from my mind, I grabbed my bag.

"Please," he begged, and snatched his pants from the floor. "Hit me back as hard as you can. You know you're stronger so you can hurt me bad."

I had planned to clock him on my way out, but changed my mind when he asked for it. If I hit him, it would mean to him we'd achieved parity and there was a chance everything could stay the way it was between us.

But there was no way in hell anything between us could stay the way it was.

"Please. Miriam," he tried to explain. "Wanting you just makes me crazy sometimes. It seems like everybody, including the narc guy following us in the Navigator yesterday, can have your love but me."

"And you know what, Billy Rose?" I answered, only half hearing what he'd said, "you never will."

I grabbed the keys from the dresser, the document pouch next to it, and left him struggling to get his other leg into his pants.

I ran into the hallway and pushed the elevator button. The car was stopped five floors up. I ran downstairs to the lobby, across the parking lot to the truck, unlocked the door, got in, and looked back to see Billy Rose running from the hotel lobby toward the truck, shirt in his hand.

I turned the key, gunned the motor, and sped away just as his hand touched the tailgate of the truck.

"You'll be sorry," he yelled. "You'll be fucking sorry, when you end up dead."

But I wasn't sorry. And I wasn't scared. I knew how to get back to I-15 North. Then it was a straight shot back to Nogales. Back to normalcy.

Inside the documents pouch I had money, passport, emergency information, cell phone, and maps. Even though I was still in Culiacán, my whole attitude had changed.

The city that had scared me stupid twenty-four hours before did not, now, scare me at all. I was leaving and foolishly had no fear of anything.

CHAPTER THIRTY-TWO

Habits are hard to break, so when I jumped into Shaun's truck in the hotel parking lot, I checked the instrument panel just as I do each time I get into my vehicle at work. I turned the key, the motor turned, and I detected movement in my peripheral vision. A look across the parking lot told me Billy Rose was coming toward me. A look back at the instrument gauges told me the low fuel light was lit. Approximate distance, assuming normal circumstances and not high-speed driving or stop and go traffic, fifteen miles.

I gunned the truck out of the parking lot, turned right, then opted to pass the gas station on the corner near the hotel and gas up at the next one. I drove five blocks and was in the middle of a gridlock of traffic. "Damn it," I said, hitting the steering wheel. I put the truck in reverse but the car behind me was too close to back up. There was no place to turn right and the policeman directing traffic wouldn't let me turn left across the street, stopping oncoming traffic.

Suddenly the anxiety attack Billy Rose induced the day before at the shrine of the narco saint returned with a vengeance. Glancing around, I saw police everywhere. News releases in the Mexican newspapers alleged some were also drug dealers and banditos. So seeing them didn't give me the same solace or comfort as back in the U.S. I rolled up the windows.

I looked around again, taking in my surroundings this time. As long as I had thought I was on my way home, I had been fine. Being stuck in traffic, so close to the hotel I'd just left, was a different story.

Billy Rose had been furious with me. If he ran behind the truck when I left the parking lot, he knew I was hemmed in by traffic just five blocks away. He could get to me in six or seven minutes.

I looked in the rear view mirror. I could see the hotel marquee glistening in the bright sunlight. No Vacancies.

Feeling queasy, I scanned the faces of pedestrians walking along the sidewalk for a mop of curly blond hair. Then I saw *him*.

At least I thought it was he, Mexican Joe.

Mexican Joe? I quickly looked back. He wasn't there.

"Calm down. Calm down. Calm down," I repeated three times, rapid fire. Whatever else I did, I couldn't panic.

I breathed deep, recited my relaxation chant and exhaled. My pulse slowed.

All superfluous thoughts fell away. With my mind quiet, I was able to concentrate. There was something I was missing. What was it? There'd been times in the past when I'd been looking for Mexican Joe, saw him, but sensed he'd been following me, and then he let me see him when it was convenient for him, but not convenient for me to carry out my mission. But I wasn't looking for him now. At the moment, my only mission was to get home.

Besides, the odds of him being here were astronomical, unless he *was* following me. But why would Mexican Joe follow me? Other than being a Border Patrol Agent, he didn't even know who I was. Or did he? If he and Mr. Guzman were connected in some way, as I believed, he could have told Mexican Joe about me.

My pulse raced again. I breathed deep, chanted, and relaxed more quickly this time. I reasoned my mind played tricks on me. I hadn't seen Mexican Joe at all. All I had done was get my mind off Billy Rose and, at the present time, he was the one I should be worried about.

A guy talking on a cell phone walked through my sight line. I immediately reversed the logic that had just given me peace. I thought, *He's a drug dealer; this place is called the drug capital of Sinoloa, why shouldn't Mexican Joe be here?* One and one make two.

When I was a little girl and would say that to Marty, she would answer, "One and one make two unless you're reproducing."

Thinking about Marty made me smile.

Clang! Metal crashed against the driver's side window, level with my ear.

I jumped. *Billy Rose*. I'd let him sneak up on me. How could I evade him in this traffic? I could ram the car in front of me, push it up and make room for the truck to squeeze onto the sidewalk. Then what?

I would figure that out when I saw how mad he was.

I held my breath, turned, and looked to the left.

An old man with rounded shoulders, toothless mouth, and a head full of straight black hair gathered in a ponytail at the nape of his neck, grinned at me and shook the tin can he'd just used to hit the window.

I was so glad to see him I didn't yell at him for scaring the shit out of me. I scrounged in my pockets and came up with a few pesos, rolled down the window, and gave them to him.

He thanked me, asked God to bless and protect me, and walked away.

I thanked the old man for his blessing and hoped his humble status brought God close enough to him to hear his prayer and really protect me. Then, watching the little old man walk away from me, I remembered one other thing I knew about Culiacán. Pedro Mercado, the man I rescued the morning I hiked in the mountains, lived here.

As if a Guardian Angel erased my previous fears, my spirits brightened.

"There must be a lot of good people in a city of seven hundred thousand," I said out loud. Once again calm and logical, I realized Billy Rose would never run out into the street after the truck, broadcasting the fact he'd been dumped. He wouldn't do it even though the only people who would see him were strangers and unaware of the circumstances. And he was too concerned about his appearance to run five blocks and end up panting and sweating. Both were totally out of character for him. It had been silly of me to imagine he would. If Mexican Joe were in Culiacán now, and on the same street at the exact same moment with me, it had to be a lottery winning, purely by chance coincidence, and nothing at all to do with me.

Both insights let me relax. The traffic crept by the accident causing the traffic jam. I was once again on my way home.

Soon I was close to the outskirts of town. Before me, sandwiched between the western coast of Mexico and the *Sierra Madre* Occidental mountain range, ribboned I-15 North. It stretched as far as I could see, and much farther than that was Nogales and home. My heart soared. I'd have to move from Green Valley, of course. The complex we lived in was the only one in town not a retirement village, with age restrictions. But moving was good. My new life would have new people in it.

Driving along, absorbed in arranging my new life, I thought it was a bump in the road the first time the truck lurched. It happened a second, then a third time in rapid succession. Then nothing.

The truck was out of gas.

Since I knew the truck was low on gas, I wasn't afraid or unduly alarmed. I had been so happy to get out of the traffic, out of town, I didn't stop for gas.

Billy Rose did a lot of off road driving in the desert and had had a second gas tank installed in the truck. I flipped the switch to activate the auxiliary tank.

Nothing happened.

An acid bubble burst in my stomach.

Then I remembered the gas container Billy Rose had put inside the truck; it was still there and full. The truck rolled the last few inches it would go under its own steam, while I steered it off the main road to the shoulder running alongside.

I gassed my vehicle every day at work. This would be quick, easy, and painless. I would be on my way in five minutes, tops.

As I opened the door of the truck and got out, a Jeep zoomed past, braked hard, and turned sharp to the left, went off the road into the ditch, kicked up dirt, dust, and pebbles, then came back onto the road, heading in my direction. In it were two Mexican police officers.

Pedro is here. Pedro is here. It gave little comfort, but it was the only talisman I had.

Following the taunting voice though the mountainous terrain the morning I hiked in the mountains around Nogales, I found Pedro Mercado, dehydrated and nearly dead. Marty said I saved his life so he could one day save mine.

"Yeah, right," I'd said to her.

Now the survival instinct in me needed to be fed. It latched onto Marty's words with the instinctual fervor of a newborn baby at nursing time.

The two police officers got out of the Jeep and came over to me. One was older than I was. The other was younger. They were both polite, congenial, and spoke to me in heavily accented, but understandable English.

"You guys are great for stopping," I smiled more with the delivery of that one sentence than I usually do all week. "I'll buy you a shot of tequila at Elvira's Restaurant when you cross the border into Nogales."

They looked at each other knowingly, smiled, asked my name and where I'd been.

Their male posturing chitchat annoyed me, but I smiled back and told them.

The older one said, "Lotsa bad things happen to pretty girls traveling alone. We go rest of the way if you sneak us across the border for drink at Elvira's."

They both laughed. Maybe they'd done it once or twice before.

Then the two-way radio in their Jeep signaled. One officer answered it; the other one gassed the truck.

The officer at the Jeep finished talking on the radio, called his partner aside where they conferred. When they returned, they were different. Official. One stood in front of me, his hand on the butt of his gun; the other positioned himself behind me, between the truck and me.

Fine hairs stood at attention all over my body. I knew this drill and it could bore a very deep hole.

"Is okay, *Senorita*," the one with his hand on the gun said. "You show us ID. You is going Elvira's in U.S."

"Sure," I said, a bit confused. "My name is Miriam Valencia. I have identification here." I pointed to the document pouch belted around my waist. "Can I get it?"

He nodded.

I opened the pouch, pulled out the ID, and handed it to him.

He looked at it; he looked back at me. He snickered and shook his head. "Is pretty picture, is not you. Is William Joseph Rose."

Billy Rose. I had picked up his pouch by mistake.

"My name is Miriam Valencia," I said, desperately wanting to recite my badge number along with it but knowing I must not. I wasn't part of a fraternal order of police brotherhood in Mexico, and I couldn't expect the courtesy law enforcement officials might give me in the States. I had to think fast and keep my wits about me. I'd heard the stories of Americans being jailed in other countries; I'd read the office intelligence reports of injustice and brutality. I didn't plan to become a statistic. There must be something in the truck that could prove who I was. I abruptly turned and moved toward the truck. The officer who'd been behind me was now in front holding up one hand. The other hand held his gun. I stopped.

"I'm sorry," I extended both my hands away from my body. "I should have told you what I was doing. In the glove box of the truck," I pointed, "there're papers proving who I am."

He looked at me, looked at his partner who unsnapped his holster, walked around the truck to the other side, opened the door, drew his gun, said, "do it," like in the movies.

I leaned inside the truck, opened the glove box, and took out the papers. The vehicle registration, Mexican automobile insurance, and exit visa, belonged to William Joseph Rose.

The policeman said, "Is same name."

"What is same name?" I asked, fearing I already knew.

"Is name report stolen truck." He pointed to the truck. "Is same stolen red truck. Same name is William Joseph Rose."

"I told you my name is Miriam Valencia," I tried to smile despite my stomach being in more knots than my hair when it dried and I hadn't first combed it. "I'm an American citizen."

"There, you American citizen," he nodded toward the north. "Here you pretty girl with stolen truck, no ID."

"I have the right to an attorney," I said.

"*Si, Senorita,*" he said, "in U.S."

"Then let me make a phone call to the U.S.," I insisted.

"*Si, Senorita,*" he said. "*Mañana* phone is work. You call then."

At the moment, I was too annoyed to be scared. Besides they were more interested in which one of them would drive the truck than in me. They didn't even try to frisk me. I was wearing an orange muscle-man tee shirt that hugged my body even before the temperature rose to ninety-five and I started to sweat, and a pair of khaki shorts with one side pocket, in which they'd seen me stuff my sunglasses. They could pretty much see I didn't have a weapon.

I wasn't happy. They were clearly having fun, and one of them was about to have more. They tossed a silver dollar to see which one would drive the truck back to the little out-of-the-way substation where they took me. I got in the Jeep and rode with the older officer, who lost. His dour expression matched my own.

Over the two-way radio, the two freely discussed, in Spanish, how many pesos they could get for Billy Rose's truck. It was in my best interest not to let them know I was fluent in their language. It was better to leave them secure in speaking their minds in front of me, thinking I didn't understand what they said.

If the entire police substation was the size of my living room in Green Valley, the detention cell was as big as my walk-in closet. In it were minuscule cubicles just big enough to hold a cot. They gave me a sheet to put over the stained, bare mattress. A consideration for me being a girl, I overheard them say. I asked for the toilet and was told, "out back." I decided to hold it as long as I could.

I hadn't eaten dinner the night before or breakfast that morning.

"*Siesta* time," the officer said, when I asked for lunch. "Now you sleep." They left me with a sweaty, middle-aged guard whose uniform probably fit him before he gained that last twenty pounds. His fingernails were caked with dirt and he'd apparently had his lunch, the remains of which he picked from his teeth with a penknife. He stood to meet me, stuck out a greasy hand. I touched it with my fingertips and then wiped them on my pants.

His eyes moved over my body, pausing in places he liked best. The guard sucked his teeth and smiled. "You keepin' her for yourself, Manuelito?" he said to the younger of the two officers in perfect English, without a Spanish accent.

The officer he called Manuelito, the Casanova of the group, grinned.

The two police locked me in a cubicle, closed me in the room by myself, and soon I heard them leave the station.

I couldn't sleep and wouldn't have if I could. I didn't trust the guard as far as I could throw him, and that would be nowhere. He weighed at least three hundred pounds. But I felt better alone with him than alone with him *and* the two officers. If he lost his mind and lusted into the cell, he'd have to work around too much of himself to hold a weapon and do anything to me at the same time. And I'd already sized him up. I knew a half dozen ways to hurt him bad.

Around six o'clock, the two officers returned. I heard the one called Manuelito tell the guard he wondered what the American would give for food.

The response brought a loud laugh. Though I didn't hear the response, my skin crawled.

The door to the detention room squeaked open. I held my breath. I could take down the guard, maybe even the other officer. But Manuelito was younger than me and stronger, and if he were coming after something, he wouldn't stop until he got it, whatever it took.

Light filtered through the opened door. *Cucarachas*, big enough to move my cot, skittered across the floor.

I waited. My heart rumbled like thunder in my chest. An old man carrying a tray draped with a piece of red cloth shuffled in. The smell of cilantro preceding him told me one thing: FOOD.

My stomach growled. The sound of my panting was as noisy as his steps.

The closet sized detention room had no window and a twenty-five-watt light bulb hung from the ceiling, casting more shadows than light. As the man neared, my eyes and mind made a memory connection, but skepticism prevented me from accepting the truth until he stood in front of me.

Pedro Mercado.

"*Angel, Verde.*" His instant recognition brought a big grin to his face. "Why you here?"

I explained.

He nodded but said nothing. What could he say? What could he do?

He must have felt he was letting me down. I had saved

his life; not being able to help me made him look grim.

I talked about other things to put him more at ease, asked him if he still had plans to go to North Carolina to work with his son on the pig farm.

He looked wistful. "Some day I go," sounded more like a prayer than a plan.

The guard entered. "What're you two talking about?"

Pedro kept my secret. He seemed to understand my problem might be rectified sooner if they didn't know I worked for the U.S. Border Patrol.

"I tell the *Senorita* I bring good food, she take me U.S.," Pedro said.

"You bring her the same crap you bring everybody else," the guard snorted. "And forget about trying to cross the border again. You were born here. You'll die here."

The guard sounded so hateful I threw the food at him.

He made Pedro clean it up, then left the room.

"I'm sorry," I said, ashamed I'd caused him more work.

"Is okay," he answered. "He born there. Hide here. Mean son of bitch."

"I'm sorry," I said.

He looked at me. "Is okay. One day, I cross border."

"Good luck," I said. But I wondered if being on a pig farm in North Carolina would be any better for him than where he was, now.

"I call somebody?" he asked.

I thought of Billy Rose. Since he was the reason I was being detained in the first place, he'd probably come for his truck and let me stay. "No, I don't know anyone here," I said.

Except Mexican Joe.

Why my subconscious thought of Mexican Joe was beyond my comprehension but once his name surfaced I wasn't able to shake the feeling I'd seen him earlier, during the traffic jam downtown.

No. It couldn't have been.

Those were the exact same words Marty had said when I told her that it was Mexican Joe's voice bulling me into following him, until I found Pedro.

"No," Marty had said. "It couldn't have been. Oh, it may have been the sound of his voice, but it was really fate leading you to the old man."

Then I remembered what Billy Rose said about the man following us in the Navigator. *I know who he is. He won't bother you.* Was he also talking about Mexican Joe? Maybe there really was something called fate and maybe if I submitted instead of resisted . . .

What the hell? What did I have to lose? I played the wild card. "When you were trying to cross the border, Pedro, did you ever hear of a man called Mexican Joe?" I started to describe him, but it wasn't necessary.

"*Si, Senorita,*" he smiled. "I meet this man in mountains." His small eyes beamed like halogen lights. "He find you. You save me. He big *chili*. He help."

He quickly gathered up everything he'd brought with him. "I find. He come."

"What's going on back there?" the guard yelled. "Pedro, get your ass out here."

"Pedro," I said. "Tell him . . ."

The door slammed against the wall like it had been kicked open. The guard stood there glaring. "Didn't I tell you to shut the fuck up?"

Pedro left without looking back. Any hope I had of getting home before the new millennium rested with him, but his lowered head and drooped shoulders left me with a feeling of despair.

The guard gave me a warning look then slammed the door behind them.

I stood at the door of the cubicle watching a *cucaracha* climb the wall only a few feet away, and blinked back any tears that wanted to form. I'd heard horror stories of U.S. citizens making a wrong turn in El Paso, Texas or other border towns and ending up in Mexico by mistake, then going to Mexican prison for years. Here I was, unable to prove American citizenship *and* they thought I stole a truck, which I suspected they'd trade for me any day of the week.

The way I saw it, looking through the bars of the cubicle that would be my accommodations for the night, the next day the police would sell the truck and that would be the last we would see of it. Either they would abuse me, and then put me in prison where I would stay the next few years waiting for their judicial process to work . . .

Or, Pedro would find Mexican Joe, who would come and get me.

But would he help me get home, or, make the first option of prison look good by comparison?

CHAPTER THIRTY-THREE

Seconds after the guard left my cell I heard his voice in the other room. At first I thought he was still lambasting Pedro for talking to me, then it was clear he was talking to the two officers who had returned to the station. From their discussion, the "mean son of a bitch," as Pedro called him, was leaving. A different guard had night duty.

"The *Senorita* will not like him," Manuelito said. "He farts like a dog and smells like a pig." His voice faded in and out as he spoke of the truck, a man in Hermosillo, and twenty thousand *pesos*. I missed most of the conversation, but understood the gist. They would get about two thousand dollars for the truck.

There was another voice, too, one I hadn't heard before. Then the door opened. An old man wearing dusty boots, faded brown pants, a plaid shirt, and cowboy hat stepped into the detention room. He was about sixty-five years old and his carriage and manners showed he'd once lived much better than his present circumstances allowed. He removed his hat and bowed slightly from the waist.

"None of that fancy stuff, old man," Manuelito said in Spanish. "You might bend over and not be able to get up."

"*Buenas noches, Senorita,*" the old man said, and softly closed the door.

The other guard and the police officers left the facility. Everything was quiet.

When the sun went down, the old guard went out like a light. He snored loudly when he inhaled and whistled through his teeth when he exhaled.

When I first arrived at the substation at *siesta* time, I'd been too conscious of my predicament and wary of my surroundings to sleep. But now the rhythm of the old man's loud breathing mesmerized me and I started to doze. I'd nod, lean forward, and bump my head on the bars and wake up. Then I'd fight sleep by thinking of people I usually only dream about.

I thought of Miguel's baby forever interred in his mother's womb, of Ismelda and what her last thought might have been, of Pedro and his undying faith that his life would be better if only he could get across the border. I thought about dozens of other people I've met and will never completely forget. Although I had been in Mexico only three days, their stories took on new meaning for me after having seen hungry families living in houses that could barely stand, land looking overworked and underfed, and half naked children chasing chickens and pigs.

And I had not seen the worst of it.

I dozed, leaned forward, and hit my head again, and took it as a reminder to be fair. Everything I saw in Mexico had not been impoverished. I also saw pockets of prosperity surrounded by manicured lawns so immaculate the blades of grass looked painted in by hand. And landscapes appointed with decadently opulent statues, ornaments, and enough gardeners to tend small farms. But too much money never awakened a Mexican early in the morning and said, "It's time to steal across the border. Leave everything you can't carry and go live where the language curls your tongue, and the people are likely to underpay you, then treat you like shit."

I also thought about Marty. After meeting Pedro again and discovering he knew Mexican Joe, I felt open to considering Marty's idea of fate and her belief in unseen forces influencing observable events. Maybe her ideas were grounded in something more substantial than her mind. At least I told myself this while my head smarted from the whack it'd gotten when I dozed off the last time.

Marty's ancestors came from the Mexican State of Sonora. They migrated north in the 1940s during the World War II era *Bracero* program's recruitment of Mexican agricultural workers and were given citizenship in 1986 when two million unauthorized residents were legalized. Marty was born a U.S. citizen and during my formative years she lived to forget the indignities Indians and Mexicans suffered, not memorialize them.

It was only after being diagnosed with cirrhosis of the liver that Marty opened her heart and mind to the traditional beliefs and customs of her Indian ancestors. Her new knowledge inspired her to discard most of what she learned while mainstreaming her life, yet she did not wholeheartedly endorse all the practices of the old people, either.

Marty believes everything that happened to her had a purpose. "If I hadn't lived the life I lived," she said, "I wouldn't be the person I am now."

Her present understanding of life allows her to embrace her imminent mortality, believing she will never truly die. Her theory that, "no one has escaped from this world dead or alive," confounded me until I realized she meant nature recycles people much like Goodyear recycles tires.

Following Marty's lead, I ignored my heritage when I was young. I'd say, "They're not talking about me," when I heard derogatory remarks about "wets," "spics," or "coons." But I learned from the universal oneness of meditation, it doesn't matter if my ancestors were East Indian, West Indian, or American Indian: At some point they all came from the same source.

Lately, I've begun to let myself suffer the heat of ignominy when strangers variously lump me with blacks, Hispanics, Indians, and other groups I look like I might belong to, but which they consider as "not belonging" here, and disparage with crude remarks. Feeling what each group feels enhances my sensitivity. My spirit sometimes walks with the spirit of the illegals I arrest. Even though the footprints I make do not bear the weight of their load, I make enough of an imprint that I now look back in shame at every time I said, "This is America, why don't they learn the language? Why don't they dress the part?"

That night in the cramped cubicle, fighting sleep, crunching cockroaches with my shoe, which they'd thankfully let me keep, I thought about my life, past and present, and I prayed I would soon have the future I had been daydreaming about when the truck ran out of gas.

The first guard had promised I could call the American Embassy the next morning. I had to believe I could; otherwise I couldn't have stayed the night in the cell without going berserk. As it was, I got a headache bumping my head. Finally I slid back on the cot, put my back against the wall, and fell asleep.

A little earlier, a noise in the other room had awakened me from that sleep. I know the time because I rubbed my eyes and looked at my watch. Eleven fifty-five, twenty minutes later than the last time I looked. But by the time my mind assimilated all that, the noise had stopped and I forgot why I woke up.

It was then the door to the detention room slowly opened.

A man stepped inside.

HASTA MAÑANA

Even in the dim light and shadow, I could tell it was the same man I'd seen standing on the ridge looking down his long arm at me the night I followed the horse into the canyon.

Mexican Joe. Tall. Arrogant. Blonde.

What was *he* doing here?

Then I remembered. Pedro said he would find Mexican Joe. The fact that he had to actually come to the jail to save me, had momentarily escaped me.

He came toward me. I was thankful the door was locked. "How did you get in here?" I asked. Then demanded, "Where's the guard?"

"Guard," I yelled.

"Won't do you any good," he said, speaking English and pulling a small gun out of the top of his military style boot.

I backed away.

"If I want to kill you that won't do any good either," he said. "This gun shoots darts. They pierce the skin and release a tranquilizer, which instantly knocks you out, like the guard out there. I woke him up and put him to sleep." He laughed like it was funny and looked over at the door. "That's how I got back here. That's why the guard won't come when you call."

He held up a key. "How else could I get this key to unlock your cell?"

The amazement I felt must have registered on my face.

"Do you want to get out of here or what?" he asked.

"The question is, get out of here *and* what?" I backed up against the wall. "What are you going to do with me?"

His smile was benevolent. He looked as kind as Pedro said he was. But I wasn't prepared for his response. "Smuggle you across the border, of course."

I gulped.

"You sent *Senor* Mercado for me," he said. "I guess he misunderstood. He thought you wanted to get out of here and go home."

"But I don't have a passport," I foolishly said.

"You don't need one."

I knew that!

I hope my boss Janet Reno forgives me. When what he proposed sunk in, I got a scintillating buzz all the way down to my toes. Concerned the Mexican authorities would be alerted to my disappearance from the jail and looking for me at their checkpoints, he was going to smuggle me across the border just like the people I had sworn to arrest. But as quickly as the sensation flowed through me, it stilled. I couldn't do that.

"I'll call the American Embassy in the morning," I said. "They will help."

He laughed softly. "Did you see a telephone out there anywhere? The *policia* will let you sit back here until they sell the sporty red truck you're driving, then they'll turn you loose on some back road and let you fend for yourself, or they'll lock you up in prison. Probably flip a coin to decide."

I remembered they'd tossed a silver dollar to see who would drive the truck. After twelve hours of exuding benign tolerance, I suddenly developed a lump of ice-cold fear in the bottom of my stomach, quickly freezing my belief in their good intentions.

He must have smelled the fear oozing from my pores.

"You can be home in the morning," he said. "Or, you can still be here waiting for them to bring in a phone just for you to make a call."

He started to walk away, then turned back. "Did I neglect to say that even if they do let you make a call, you're still charged with stealing the truck?" He added, "They can dismiss the charge if your boyfriend drops it, but you'll have to remain in Mexican custody until they find him."

What Mexican Joe said was true. If I wanted to get out of Mexico and home in the near future, I had to go then, and with him. My only consolation was in knowing the Mexican police hadn't fingerprinted or photographed me. If I just disappeared, there'd be no official record of me having been there.

I didn't worry if Mexican Joe could get me across the border; he did it a couple of times a day. My concern was that I really didn't know anything about Mexican Joe except what Pedro Mercado and Billy Rose had told me. I had to rely on their judgment to decide whether or not to trust him but first I had to decide which one told me the truth. When I closed my eyes and thought of Pedro, his aura appeared before me as whispery soft as angel hair. Though I secretly wanted to believe Billy Rose would not mislead me, when I closed my eyes and thought of him, his aura loomed over me as though conjured up by a Mojo spell.

"It's your call, Miss Valencia," Mexican Joe said. "The guard will wake up in a few minutes. I can't give him another tranquilizer, it might kill him. If you're going, we have to leave now."

He knew my name. Pedro didn't know it to tell him. But that wasn't what unsettled me. What unsettled me was this: I wanted to go home more than I've ever wanted to do anything in my life. The irony of it being I'd have to do it with a man I'd maliciously stalked not more than a week before. Marty would undoubtedly say it was poetic justice, but it didn't feel right to me.

In the end, the bottom-line set the course. Even if they let me talk to someone at the American Embassy, Billy Rose would have to cooperate for the charges to be dropped.

How long would that take? As long as it took to sate his need for revenge.

Expediency cast the winning ballot.

When Mexican Joe unlocked the door and pulled it open, I walked through.

CHAPTER THIRTY-FOUR

Mexican Joe and I left the substation at midnight. The air was muggy and hot, but we were just shy of the Tropic of Cancer in mid-August and the heat and humidity were expected. Shaun's red truck was not in the parking lot where it had been parked at noon. That, too, was expected.

We got into a Jeep, which was probably green when the layers of dirt were washed off. "I thought you drove a black Navigator," I said.

"Why'd you think that?"

"One followed us yesterday, the day before, now. I thought it was you."

The door to the jeep was still open; the dome light was on. When Mexican Joe looked over at me, secret knowledge registered in his gray-green eyes.

"Buckle up," he said. "We have a long ride."

He said nothing more for the next two hours.

Culiacán to Guyama is about three hundred miles. According to the trip meter that he'd reset when we started, we were more than halfway there when I asked, "Where are we?"

"We're in my Jeep on the road to the States," Mexican Joe said.

Dumb question. Smart answer.

"My mother said you saved my life at the train station on Sale Day," I next said. "Is that what you were doing?"

He said nothing.

"Marty—I call my mother Marty—said one day I'll save your life because you saved mine. Do you believe it, too?"

"It doesn't much matter whether I believe it or not," he said without explanation. He did accelerate, though, and turned the air conditioner up high; the noise from the fan made normal conversation difficult.

The darkened landscape zipped by so fast I couldn't isolate known landmarks, but I knew for sure we were not returning to Nogales via I-15 North, at least we hadn't been on it since I started noticing. Soon the outside temperature dropped, and he turned off the air conditioner.

"What'll you do if we're stopped?"

"Here or there?" he asked.

"Here." I said. "In Mexico."

"It depends on who stops us." He never took his eyes from the road, which was good. It was rutted with lots of dips and curves.

"Okay." I silently renewed my determination to engage him in meaningful conversation. There were so many things I wanted to ask him. They were questions I had to creep up on gingerly. "What if we're stopped crossing the border into the U.S.?"

"It depends on who stops us."

Absolutely.

I looked at him.

He looked at me. In the dim light, I don't think he saw the consternation in my face, or he saw it and didn't care.

"Get some rest," he said. "We have a few more hours before we get where we're going and you don't have to make idle chitchat just to be sociable."

I couldn't be dismissed so easily. "Would you like for me to drive?"

"No," he said. "I've seen you drive. What I'd really like is for you to be quiet. I'm working on a problem. Silence would help."

HASTA MAÑANA

He could have smacked me and it probably wouldn't have hurt my feelings more. Of all the things I'd thought since he walked into the detention room at the substation, it hadn't occurred to me I was a bother to him.

"If I'm interfering with 'business as usual,' " I said, a bit terse, perhaps, for someone in my shoes, "I can go the rest of the way on my own. Other people manage to find their way across the border."

He slammed the brakes hard.

I braced myself on the dashboard. The Jeep stopped.

I clenched my teeth. "What did you do that for?"

"You said you could manage on your own," he said. "This is as good a place as any to get out and start."

From the distance recorded on the trip meter, we should be in the Mexican State of Sonora, meaning we were probably about a two-hour drive from Nogales. I knew enough about astronomy to find my way north by looking up at the night sky, but a two-hour drive could easily turn into a week-long walk, much of it under the cloak of darkness. If I let myself, I could sleep. Then the two hours would stretch before me like a blank canvas to be filled with images from my dreams. I didn't tell him that, though. I simply slid down in the corner of my seat and closed my eyes. When I opened them again I was being shaken awake.

"You're home," he said. "Wake up."

I yawned, rubbed my eyes, and prepared myself for the walk. But when I became oriented to the surroundings, I saw I really was home, in the parking lot of the apartment complex in Green Valley. He had sneaked me across the border and I had slept right through it.

"There are lots of places you can drive across the border," he said, answering my unasked question. "If you have the right vehicle and enough gas. But I guess that's why you had the truck retrofitted with a second tank."

"That's not why . . ." I stopped mid-sentence because it very well could have been the reason Billy Rose put the other tank in the truck. I'd taken his word for so long I didn't always ask the right questions when he explained things to me. Not a good practice. I'd had proof of it in the past twenty-four hours.

"Thank you," I said. "Can I pay you something for your time and trouble?"

"No."

"At least let me pay for the gas." I reached for the leather pouch and remembered the Mexican police officers had it. They had authentic ID, thousands of dollars in traveler's checks, and the truck. All in all, a good day's haul. I knew the INS did not assess fines that high when aliens crossed illegally and were able to stay here long enough to apply for residency. I'd more than paid the fine. Now when I think about my illegal cross of the border, I'll think of it as expensive, not shameful.

"Sorry," I said. "If you wait until I go inside, I can get money to pay for your kindness."

"Miss Valencia," he said softly.

"Yes, Mister, what *is* your name?"

"What have you been calling me?"

I thought back. I had referred to him many times as Mexican Joe, but I had never actually called him anything to his face. I said as much.

"It seems to work," he said. "Let's not spoil it. If you don't know who I am, you can't ever tell who brought you across the border. And by the way, you can't pay for kindness. It's freely given. I really do have to go now."

He drove away, braked, and then backed back to where I

stood. "In case you're afraid to go inside, he's still in Mexico."

Billy Rose hadn't even been on my mind. I didn't think he had returned from Guadalajara because he had business there. Nothing interfered with business. He also kept a lock box there, in the *Banco de Mexico*, for emergencies. In it he kept money and ID.

When Mexican Joe sped away, the sun was burning off the fog. It would be a hot Friday. I wasn't due back at work until the next day, Saturday, so I would spend the rest of today looking for a place to live.

I promised myself, even if I had to stay in a motel for a few days, I would be out of the apartment when Billy Rose returned on Sunday.

That was the plan.

CHAPTER THIRTY-FIVE

Early Saturday morning I walked out of the apartment, locked the door, collected my things on the landing, then looked out over the pool. Shaun's red truck was in the parking lot.

My heart raced. My breath caught in my throat. I had thought I had another day to move out of the apartment before Billy Rose returned. I wasn't ready to see him, but I wasn't going to avoid him either. This confrontation had to happen. It would just be sooner rather than later.

I walked down the sixteen steps to the ground, around the pool, and past the colony of Africanized honeybees. I told myself Billy Rose didn't frighten me, but my fingers knew different and quietly unsnapped my holster. My hand came to rest on the butt of my gun just as it would in any potentially dangerous situation.

When I got close enough, I saw Shaun's truck was parked in Mr. Kim's parking space. I walked slower. If Billy Rose were asleep in the front seat, I'd walk on by. Let Mr. Kim wake him if he wanted his parking space. If he were not in the truck, I would move it to the right parking space then leave for work.

I had both scenarios worked out in my mind, but I noticed my feet were not in a hurry to get to the truck, either way.

It was six o'clock in the morning. The windows of the truck were fogged from temperature inversion. The hood was hot to my touch. I slowly opened the driver's door and a piece of white paper floated down to my feet. I looked inside the truck, front and back. It was empty. I bent down and picked up the paper. It was a note, written by a stranger's hand.

> Thought you might want the truck.
> P. S. Don't blame yourself for what happened. It wasn't your fault.

What had happened? Well, actually, a lot had happened but I couldn't think of anything for which I should take blame. I crumpled the paper, pulled at the ashtray to open it and stuff the paper in, but it was stuck. I jerked. The ashtray zipped out, spilling a man's pinky ring and ashes all over the truck floor. I jumped back to keep them from getting on my uniform and cursed. The ring looked familiar, but what I instantly remembered was Billy Rose's lovebirds.

Billy Rose had a pair of lovebirds when we lived next door to each other in Tucson. One of the lovebirds died. Billy Rose said the other bird would be sad and die, too, because lovebirds mate for life. The remaining bird didn't look lovesick to me, but sure enough, she was dead later that day. "I told you," he said. "She pined away for him."

Billy Rose burned both birds in the backyard barbecue pit and ran around the yard, ashes flying in the wind. When he finished, he was covered with sooty residue. He said, "We should be cremated when we die and our ashes mingled so we'll be together forever." I had been ten years old at the time and the incident didn't seem nearly as weird as it did when I relived it this morning, standing with the truck's ashtray in my hand.

The weird feeling changed to a chill, consuming my senses and conversely making me hot. *Someone is dead.*

Beads of sweat pimpled my forehead, neck, and chest.

Marty.

I snatched out my cell phone and punched her speed-dial number. She answered on the sixth ring. I giggled childishly.

"It's a good thing I have caller ID," she said, "or I'd have let it ring. Why're you calling me so early in the morning? And when did you get back from Mexico?"

I was embarrassed to say I'd forgotten to call her, so I just told her I'd come back early and spent the day looking for a place of my own.

She said, "It's about damn time."

We arranged to have dinner later. I would tell her what happened then.

CHAPTER THIRTY-SIX

Two weeks after first arriving in Nogales, the Agent in Charge greeted us at early morning muster with, "We've had a homicide." It couldn't have gotten quieter in the room if a magician had cast a spell. Most never see a killing, but death and dying are two things that are always on the mind of law enforcement officials. Suddenly the fear came home to roost. It stunned us silent.

The first morning the H word was mentioned, the Agent in Charge was an expert at being inappropriate. He thought it was funny to announce the killing of a rattlesnake that way.

We thought he was an ass.

But this morning the Agent in Charge was a no nonsense person. When he said, "Two nights ago there was a homicide," everyone looked around to see who was missing from the room. Of course, he could have meant one of our agents had killed someone, but our thoughts first turned to our own.

He didn't give us a chance to speculate about the status of the agents who weren't in the room. "This morning at 0600 hours," he stopped and cleared his throat. "The body of Enrique Guzman was discovered at the Sasabe port of entry."

"Nooo," I heard someone moan, but didn't realize it was me until the agent sitting next to me grabbed my hand and squeezed it hard. I was the only woman in the room, but I wasn't the only one to cry.

"Mr. Guzman was shot in the back at least twenty-four hours earlier," he said. "He was killed someplace else, then brought to Sasabe to be found."

Sasabe was a minor port of entry, an out-of-the-way place manned during the day, but closed at night.

"The son of a bitch who did it cut off Mr. Guzman's finger," he blew his nose. "You wouldn't have had a reason to know this," he continued, "and I'm only telling you now because I helped start the rumors floating around. Mr. Guzman was a good and honest man."

He looked out of the window until he found the strength to go on. "He was a highly decorated Marine. He was stationed in Southeast Asia and worked in the military anti-drug section. The Border Patrol was lucky to get him when he quit the military. He was working undercover in conjunction with the DEA. The rumor you heard about him stealing drugs from the Miami Police Department evidence room was part of his cover. He recently returned here from the East Coast where that semi was stopped in the New Jersey. He'd followed the drugs from Mexico but lost them when they, too, were stolen from a police department evidence room later that day." He spoke as though he'd memorized a news release.

"Three days ago Mr. Guzman went to Culiacán. All we know for sure is he and his undercover DEA partner were supposed to rendezvous with a drug dealer, a behind-the-scenes broker, in Guadalajara."

He said more, I'm sure, but I wasn't listening. All I wanted to do was to get out of the room. When we finally did leave, my feelings were cloaked in a façade of benign grief. I was still on duty. I had to work, had to function like a flesh and blood agent, despite feeling like a hollow shell.

When my shift was over, I got in Shaun's truck, put in a

tribal music CD, and drove to my favorite ridge to be alone. I needed to understand why I cried out like I did when I learned Mr. Guzman was dead. I really wasn't in love with him, as Billy Rose had tried to imply. There was a fleeting second, though, when I'd been drawn to him, or thought he was drawn to me, but in later weeks I reconsidered and thought I misjudged either the moment or his intent.

So I must have cried out because of an accumulation of everything that had happened the previous three days, and my nervous system couldn't take one more thing. It had to be that. He was my journeyman and nothing more. We weren't friends. I never even bought the Tequila I'd promised him for not telling the other agents he'd seen me cry. Well, they saw me cry today. I didn't give a damn.

I climbed to the top of the ridge, faced the setting sun, then sat with legs crossed, breathed deeply, and began to meditate. I thought about all the bad things that had happened to me when I was young; how they pushed me further and further into the darkness of my own soul, away from other people because I always feared a breech of trust. But I had survived that; I could survive this, too.

Then I focused on Mr. Guzman. He didn't ask me if I needed help; he hadn't listened when my words and my actions said, "I can do it by myself." He was a good journeyman. He knew what I needed and he took the raw material the Academy graduated and inside of two weeks fashioned me into a good agent. He was a hard taskmaster and, like a good father, he demanded from me the near perfection he demanded of himself. I will never forget him for what he did. I will never let him down. He would have been a good person to have in my life for a long time to come.

I sat on the ridge and meditated until I realized I had cried out in the muster room because I missed what could have been. He could have been a friend.

Then I climbed down.

When I got back to Shaun's truck, Mexican Joe stood next to it.

"You need another truck," he said. "Fire engine red is too easy to find."

He tried to smile. I could tell his heart wasn't in it, but it wouldn't have mattered.

"You killed him," I yelled, then lunged for his throat, both hands outstretched. "You knew what he was that night in the canyon," I screamed. "You let him go so you could kill him later."

He grabbed my hand, swung me around, grabbed the other hand, and crisscrossed my arms around my body, the restraint of a crazy person. Then he pushed me forward until I was sandwiched between him and the truck. The running board prevented me from using my feet. He prevented me from using my hands. My mouth was away from his body.

"Let me go, you son of a bitch." When I jerked against him, he tightened his hold. The blood flowing to my arms became constricted. They went numb.

"You've got to calm down," he said. "I don't want to hurt you, but I'm not going to let you hurt me, either."

I stopped struggling.

"You're right," he said. "I let him go that night because I knew who he was."

He stumbled over a couple of words, but quickly recovered. "But I didn't kill him," he said. "I was getting you out of jail."

I answered by trying to wrench free.

He locked his arms. "I will let you go," he said. "But promise me you'll call the station and ask someone the time of death."

"I promise you the animal who did this is going to pay."

"That's not the promise I need," his voice broke. "Promise."

I stood still. I knew he wouldn't tell me to call the station if he couldn't prove what he'd said. But I stopped struggling because Mexican Joe was obviously upset by Mr. Guzman's death. A wild notion formed in my mind. "You're DEA, aren't you?"

"I can't tell you that."

"You were his undercover partner, weren't you?"

His breath came rough. A man trying not to cry. "Even if it's true, I couldn't tell you." Hot tears fell on my back. He brushed them away in my hair.

It had been quite a few seconds since I stopped fighting him, but he leaned in to me as though he needed a crutch to stand.

He cleared his throat. "I can tell you this. Enrique Guzman thought you were a fine agent. He had a daughter once. He thought she might have been much like you if she had lived. He asked me to look out for you if anything happened to him."

He laughed lightly. "Personally? I think you can take care of yourself."

"He once told me things were not what they seemed," I said. "Was that what he meant?"

"Maybe. Maybe not. A lot of things are not what they seem. Sometimes you just have to wait until tomorrow to find out what happened today."

He released his hold on me.

I rubbed my arms and turned toward him. In his eyes I saw the man Pedro Mercado knew.

"He cared for you," he said. "He only knew you for a short time, but he cared deeply. He said you were like a wild animal who licked her own wounds."

I must have grimaced.

"That's not bad," he said. "It's sad, but it's not bad."

"What else did he say?"

"He said in some ways you were still very much a child."

"Maybe I was, then," I said. "But now I feel like an old woman with Alzheimer's. I don't know where to turn or who to trust. What's real and what's not."

"I know," he said and I believed he did. I just didn't know how he knew.

He read the question in my face, my eyes.

"War changes people," he answered. "And what we wage here on the border is war. A never-ending war we have no chance in hell of winning. The drugs aren't going to stop coming any more than the people, until there's nothing left here to spoil.

"You have to learn to trust yourself, Miriam. When you can do that, something inside of you will tell you who else to trust."

He turned and walked away.

"What do I call you?" I yelled after him, doubting I would talk to him again.

"Why not call me Jon?" he said. "That's what my mother named me."

"Jon? Where did Mexican Joe come from?"

He walked back to me.

Dusk was fading into night but I could clearly see his face. His eyes seemed to indicate he sifted through what he could tell me and what he would, much like Mr. Guzman had done when I asked questions he never intended to fully answer either.

"I heard once, 'Mexican Joe' was the name the DEA gave a special project they were undertaking to stop a military man turned drug trafficker named Joseph DiRossi. He was in Southeast Asia when Enrique was there. DiRossi was stationed in Arizona when he re-upped the last time. Once stateside, he hooked up with the Mexican cartel, but his own addictions had made him unreliable and he had to 're-tire' from the business. He was always small potatoes, though, compared to what his son has become."

My mind made mental calculations for the number of years he was talking about. "You don't expect me to believe our government would spend hundreds of thousands of dollars to take down one drug dealer?"

"Our government spends a lot more than that paying agents to return illegals who re-cross the border before the agent gets back to the station," he said.

I shut up and listened. He said the DEA snooped and trailed the son and paid informers but had nothing concrete. "No evidence. No arrest."

"This man was one of those computer whiz kids and could have gone the way of Bill Gates and become a legitimate billionaire, but he walked on the other side of the street. He lives like an ordinary guy but he's got millions stashed away.

"Sound like anybody you know?"

"No," I said, "not really. I don't know any rich people."

"Well," he said, "the DEA knows who he is. But that's not what you asked me, is it? My answer is this. If I worked on that DEA project, I'd call myself Mexican Joe to remind me every second of every day what I'd sworn to do. If I didn't work for DEA, I'd call myself that anyway because I think it's a cool name."

"What is the drug dealer's name?"

"He calls himself a broker, and that's why it's hard to catch him. He doesn't carry his inventory around in a car with darkly tinted windows. His name is W. Joseph DiRossi."

"I've got to go," I said, and abruptly turned toward the truck.

"Wait," he said.

"No," I turned back. "You wait. I know what you're trying to do. I know Mr. Rose was stationed in Southeast Asia. I know he was trying to get away from a bad extended family image back east and changed his name from DiRossi to Rose. You're trying to poison my mind with lies and innuendoes when you're nothing but a drug smuggler yourself."

"I can show you this," he said, "but then I'll have to kill you." He faked a laugh, reached into his boot and pulled out a DEA star.

He looked triumphant but all he did was prove what I already knew. He was Mr. Guzman's partner. But he didn't prove he wasn't a liar or a drug smuggler.

"You showed it to me. If you shoot me, it'll have to be in the back," I said. "Like you did Mr. Guzman."

I turned back to the truck, got in, and drove away.

CHAPTER THIRTY-SEVEN

The sun went down and stars softly lit the horizon on my drive back to Green Valley. It was too late to move my things to a motel and I was too emotionally exhausted to care if Billy Rose came back while I was still in the apartment. I would call Marty and beg off dinner, and then I would go to sleep. It was the best thing I could do for myself at the time.

Upon entering the apartment, I saw the red light blinking on the answering machine. There were six messages. I thought they were probably from some of the agents at the station calling to check on me, but I played the messages back anyway.

The first message was from Marty. Her voice chilled me. Her words, "I don't feel well enough to eat," alarmed me. Marty didn't have a hearty appetite, but she didn't pass up dinner out.

The second message was from the station. "Your mother called for you."

The third message was from Mrs. Kim. "Marty not good. I tell her call 911."

The fourth message was from the Ward Clerk at Tucson General Hospital. "I promised I'd call if Marty ever ended up here without you."

The fifth message was from Father Angelo. "Miriam, I'm at the Hospital. Marty has received the Holy Sacrament. You'd better come now."

The last message was from Billy Rose.

I didn't wait to hear what he had to say.

CHAPTER THIRTY-EIGHT

During the five months I'd lived in Green Valley, I'd developed a nodding acquaintance with most of the officers of the Pima County Sheriff's Department when we'd stopped at the Circle K for coffee. I called the dispatcher from my cell phone as I ran down the stairs to the truck. I told them where I was starting from, where I was going, and why. I described my truck, gave them the license plate number then told them to stay the hell out of my way or be prepared to shoot me dead.

I headed for I-19 North, the fastest route to Tucson. Officer Pete Ramirez got there before me and parked his Sheriff's Department car across the entrance ramp, stopping traffic. He made me park the truck on the side of the road and get in his car. He took me to Tucson faster than I would have gotten there if I had driven myself.

When I got to Marty's room, my heart felt useless in my chest. It was beating but I was so weak I wasn't at all sure it pumped blood. I forced a mask of optimism on my face and entered.

Marty was propped up with pillows at her back. In the soft glow of the nightlight, Miguel held her hands and spoke to her softly in Spanish. Father Angelo was there, the Blessed Sacrament in his hand. Marty didn't look like she was dying. My heart knew she was.

I sent everyone from the room so we could be alone.

Marty didn't waste time reassuring me or trying to tell me everything would be all right. She needed to unburden her soul and she got right to the point.

"I know what that man did to you," she said, her voice weak, her eyes clear and strong. Her face showed age but neither distress nor disease registered. She was wearing the black peignoir she had pre-packed in her emergency bag and her birth blanket was wrapped around her shoulders like a shawl. Her hair was still waist length and luxurious. She was a vision reminiscent of an Indian princess or a Mexican *senorita*. I felt my heart would break, but what it did do was take a picture of her then, so I would carry the vision in my mind forever.

"What man?" I asked. I knew what man. "What are you talking about?" I knew what she was talking about.

"I know how Shaun got inside you," she said.

My knees went weak. *Not now. Please God, not now. Let it go unsaid.*

"I've known for a year now," she continued, "but I let that half-a-man, William Joseph, strut around claiming grief he never showed. He came to see me earlier today. I threw him out, but I ate the fruit he brought me."

Marty reached for my hand. "I hoped you would find this out for yourself, but William Joseph was in on it, too. He wanted to go to that concert. His father told him he'd have to earn his money, then told him how he could do it."

This wasn't the confession I was expecting. My mentor had been found dead that morning. My mother chose the event of her deathbed to slough off a wound I let heal with the thorn still inside. But there was more. She was telling me Billy Rose betrayed me as far back as eighteen years ago and had bullied her today. How much more could I take?

My knees collapsed, I slumped to the floor and rested my head on her bed. "You don't have to tell me your part," I said, my head buried in her covers.

"Yes, I do," she said. "This may be the last thing I ever do, but I can't die without telling you what I did."

I didn't want her to tell me what she had done; Mr. Rose already told me. And Marty was right. I should have figured out Billy Rose was involved. Why else would I have been at the Rose house when Billy Rose and his mother were away if someone had not carefully orchestrated the movement of all the players?

When I looked back to Marty, I didn't know if she was crying or if her eyes just looked that way through my own tears.

I inherited Marty's long hair. I also had the fire from her eyes, which could promise passion or guarantee hate. Mr. Rose had wanted Marty in the worst way. I remember she called him, "a junkyard dog, sniffing around a T-bone steak he's never going to eat."

Uncle Connie had laughed. "That's the truth," he said. "And it'd better be true."

She'd said to Connie, "You don't have to worry. It ain't going to happen." What she hadn't understood was this: Connie didn't want it to happen because he had made a bet with the junkyard dog and Connie's prized acquisition, the sawed off shotgun, was the ante.

Marty adjusted her body, sniffed into her handkerchief, and continued her story. "That asshole, Connie, told the junkyard dog he'd give him that sawed off shotgun of his if he ever got close enough to sniff that 'hot Mexican pussy.' "

"Marty," I said. "You don't have to tell me this."

"Yes, I do," she said. "I may not have been much of a mother, but I was a mother. Something bad happened to my daughter and it happened when I was sliding down the wrong side of a mountain. It was all I could do to hang on myself and I missed all the signs telling me something was wrong with my baby.

"I just want to be able to die with you knowing I fixed it." She nodded her head, then continued her story.

"I knew the two men were planning something. I just didn't know what they planned. See, I thought they were talking about me, but . . . ."

She couldn't finish the sentence, but I knew its end. "They were talking about me."

"Yes," she sobbed. "My pretty baby, they were talking about you. And me, 'Miss Hot Stuff,' thought I was the prize. Then Connie got shipped out and I forgot all about it."

Marty wiped her eyes. "Remember? You went through that period when you locked yourself in your room for days at a time and talked to me like I was a stranger, if you said anything at all. My instincts told me something had happened to you, but I didn't think I could deal with it if I knew for sure. So I didn't prod like I should have. Then you told me you were pregnant and I thought, 'That's it. That's her problem. We can fix it.'

"It hurt me, you know, not to be a part of my grandson's life, but I was such a rotten mother, I let it go. But when Shaun died, I went over there to tell them, no, beg them to let him be buried with his birth blanket."

Marty had taught me about the birth blanket, the first cloth used to swaddle the newborn. As long as the mere fibers of the cloth exist, the pure essence of one's life first breathed into it, is still there. When you die, the birth blanket is to be buried with you to complete your circle.

Marty said, "Well, Mr. High and Mighty, William Joseph Rose, Sr., decided he wasn't going to let 'no son of mine be buried like a heathen.'

"I was dumbstruck," she said, and she looked so even then.

" 'No son of yours?' I said. 'You mean grandson, don't you?' He laughed. Told me Shaun was *his* son and if I made a stink about it he would broadcast all over the neighborhood you seduced him when he was drunk. He called you a 'half-breed Mexican whore.'

"I told him whores got paid. He said, 'She did get paid.' Then he told me about the money that spineless bastard son of his got for 'brokering the deal.'

"His wife was there when he told me this. He made her verify it. Made her tell how she'd come in and saw him on top of you, you screaming and fighting. Made her tell me Connie sent him that shotgun by special delivery. I never heard from the bastard after he left here, and he sent him a gun for raping you."

Silent tears ran down her cheeks. She was remembering her encounter with Mr. Rose and it hurt her all over again. "He got up, took his shotgun from the cabinet and shoved it in my face, for me to see his prize. When he needed another drink, he sent his wife into the kitchen to get it. She brought it back and he lay the gun on the table to take the drink."

Marty stopped crying.

I was burning with hate by then. I wanted to kill him myself. Or at least go to the grave, dig him up, and desecrate his body.

Marty blew her nose and sniffed. "Father Angelo got you out of town, you know. He said it was better for you, better for me, better for the baby."

"You've known this for a year, Marty. Why didn't you say something?"

"I said nothing," she said. "But you gotta know I did

something, Baby. I fixed it for you."

She didn't have to tell me what she did. I already knew. Billy Rose had known, too. "Funny," he had said at the time. "Blasting him to smithereens seems more your mother's style than mine."

Marty started talking again. "I told that junkyard dog, 'You got Shaun's baby things. A grandmother deserves something. I want his birth blanket to keep with me. To take with me when I die, 'cause maybe I'll see him again. I won't be in his memory, but his smell is meshed in that birth blanket. He'll know I'm one of his own. Please,' I begged him, 'I'll do anything.'

"He misunderstood my meaning and laughed at me. Told me to get the hell out of his house. I was too late to exchange favors. There was a time when he would have given it to me for a little of my 'Mexican consideration,' but 'your stuff's too old and worn out now,' he said. 'Ain't worth shit.'

"I told him to consider this, and gave him the finger."

Her tears were gone. Her eyes were clear again. "That son of a bitch slapped me across the face and turned his fucking back on me. I told him 'my Mexican consideration wouldn't appreciate your little jumping bean,' while I eased two shells in the chamber of that shotgun.

"When Mr. Junkyard Dog turned back to say whatever he was to say, I pulled the trigger and he never said nothing, ever again."

"Mrs. Rose was there," I said. "What did she say?"

"What do you think she said? 'I should have done that a long time ago.' She's the one who thought up the story to tell the police, said they would never arrest her, even threw herself against the wall a couple of times so her face would be bruised. Baby, why didn't you ever say anything to me? Tell me what he did?"

"I was waiting for you to say something to me. The day he raped me, he told me you sold me to him. That's what I thought you were going to confess to me."

"How could you think that?"

"I knew money was tight, Uncle Connie leaving so abruptly and everything. Sometimes you got creative to make ends meet. How was I to know for sure you didn't do this without asking you, and I didn't want to know for sure if the answer was yes."

Marty sobbed pitifully. "I did so much wrong it was only natural you'd think I'd do that. But I didn't, Honey. I swear I'd never do that to you."

"I know that now, Marty. But I was only thirteen, I didn't know then. Besides, it was over. 'Don't cry over spilt milk' you always told me. So I didn't."

"That bastard told you I sold you to him?" She got feisty. "Now I got a reason to die," she said. "If I have to spend the rest of eternity looking for him, I'll make him pay for hardening your heart toward me."

Marty closed her eyes and lay back on the pillow.

"Marty," I whispered urgently. "Marty."

I shook her. "Mama? Mama!"

She opened her eyes. "I haven't heard you call me Mama since you were five years old," she said. "I guess I'd better die now while you love me."

I smiled into her eyes. "I've always loved you."

She looked deep into my eyes, her eyes twinkling with mischief. "You say that now. When you find out what I did for Miguel you might think differently."

She sighed. She struggled to whisper. "Go to Father Angelo if you have troubles. He's been my friend all my life. He knows all my secrets."

She smiled at me sweetly and then she died.

CHAPTER THIRTY-NINE

Marty once told me she wanted to die before her features changed so much she wouldn't recognize the woman staring back at her from the mirror. She got her wish. I didn't get mine, though; my wish was that she wouldn't die at all. When death came to her, I could barely breathe and I didn't quite know how my heart would carry the load of more pain, but it was not exempted from the journey.

When Marty died, Miguel ran into the room behind the hospital staff that had been alerted by the monitors strapped to Marty's chest. He was openly distraught, but I think Miguel also felt the grief of his own family dying as much as he was grieving for his newly adopted aunt. He desperately clung to me until Father Angelo reassured him he'd still be safe, then took him away.

Later that night, I slept fitfully. And perhaps the thrashing, twisting, and turning sloughed off my old skin and somehow metamorphosed me into a new being, inside out. I do know this: when I arose Sunday morning, I saw many things with a different mind.

My becoming a Border Patrol Agent was not intended to be a permanent career move. Billy Rose leased a furnished apartment and we brought only clothing, linen, and a few kitchen essentials from California. The rest of my belongings, including my car, were locked in Golden State Storage in Oxnard. There was still a teacher shortage, and I could always go back to my job teaching.

So when I went outside Sunday morning, felt the hot sun

on my face, heard my neighbors waking up, smelled Mrs. Kim's coffee brewing in her apartment, I knew the world had not changed substantially and my problems had not gone away. It was then I decided Billy Rose was leaving the apartment, not me. He was hardly ever there, anyway. I didn't have the time or the energy to look for another place.

While I put the last of his things in the truck, the locksmith re-keyed the locks. Then I went to the apartment manager to give her a copy of the new key.

"I've changed the lock on apartment 3125," I said.

She wasn't hearing me because she answered, "You can't do that."

I held up the brand new key for her to see. "I already have. Billy Rose doesn't have this key," I added, "and he's not to have access to the apartment."

"His name is on the lease," she reached for the key. "I can't deny him access unless he breaks some of our rules."

Just as her hand touched it, I retracted the key. "You can't allow him access if you don't have a key, which you don't, and you won't, unless . . ."

"You've got to give me a key," she insisted, with an attitude. "In case of emergencies."

I put the key back on the ring, with an equal and opposite attitude. "If there's an emergency and I'm inside, I'll let you in. If there's an emergency and I'm not here, I'll let you in when I get back. If Billy Rose contacts you, please tell him his things are at his mother's house."

"I don't know," she said, still obsessing about the key. "The management company is not going to be happy about this key situation when I tell them."

"Then don't tell them."

"Oh, I have to report any irregularities."

I didn't know if the complex had illegals keeping the

grounds or not, but being so close to the border, I took an educated guess.

"Look, lady," I said. "My mother just died and I'm living with a world class jerk. If you think the management company is going to be unhappy about a key, which they don't have to know about, then think how unhappy they'll be when I round up all the suspicious people I see working on the grounds and make them prove citizenship."

The manager suddenly remembered, in cases of domestic violence she could be creative, "at least for a while," which I loosely translated to mean until Billy Rose made a bigger fuss than I just did. But it would buy me time.

We smiled at each other, said good-bye, then she probably called me "bitch," just like I did her as soon as we were out of earshot of each other.

Mrs. Rose said she was sorry about Marty. She may have been sorry to hear about Billy Rose and me, too, if I had told her, but I didn't. I figured she'd probably figure it out from the bags of clothes.

While at the house, I asked Mrs. Rose for the shotgun Marty used to kill her husband.

"I thought Martina would get around to telling you before she died." She unlocked the gun cabinet, took out the shotgun, and handed it to me. "Did she tell you about Billy, too?"

"Yes."

"I see." She retracted her hand before I touched the gun, broke the gun down and checked for shells, then she gave it to me. But she didn't look me in the eye.

I wasn't sure whether she thought I was going to shoot her, Billy Rose, or myself if she left shells in the gun. I didn't embarrass her by asking. And I didn't frighten her by declaring I could get more shells within minutes of leaving her house.

After I left the Rose house, I went shopping for Marty. She would be cremated. Still I splurged on everything. And because Father Angelo didn't know Marty was being cremated, I also bought a casket to inter her remains.

It was already dark when I arrived at the apartment Sunday night. The red blinking light of the answering machine caught my eye as soon as I entered the room. Eight messages, seven new and one saved. Most were condolences. The Agent in Charge let me know Mr. Guzman's body was shipped home for burial. Father Angelo confirmed Monday noon for the memorial service. Marty's lawyer said, "Be prepared. Marty didn't dispose of her possessions in the customary manner."

Translation: She left everything to Miguel. But I was okay with it.

The last message was the one I had saved the night before, from Billy Rose. He said, "Did you like my present?"

What present? I didn't get a present. UPS probably left it at the manager's office. That was okay, too. She could have it for the trouble he would cause for her.

CHAPTER FORTY

Marty had pre-written her funeral service, including the eulogy, which removed that emotional strain from my heart. Still, I wasn't ready to let her go. So much had not happened between us, as mother and daughter; now it never would.

Marty promised me she would always be near, like the old ones who give me so much strength and comfort. The only thing is, I never actually knew any of them and could therefore imagine—no, believe—they were wise, strong, and out there in the heavens.

On the other hand, I knew Marty well. I knew her feet were made of clay from the many times I washed off the muck when she'd stood too long in it. I used to wonder if I could trust that her spirit would transmute into something capable of giving wise counsel. When she died, I didn't see her spirit float from her body and up into the heavens, but I have no doubts it did. And I will call upon her counsel every day I live.

It wasn't easy for me to do, but I combed Marty's hair, plaited the one long braid she preferred and laid it over her shoulder. I put make-up on her face and dressed her in a beautiful black peignoir, made of hand tatted Spanish lace. I closed the front of the gown, at her breast, with the two-thousand-dollar lacquered beetle pin Billy Rose brought from Brazil, and Marty secretly coveted.

I disassembled the shotgun she killed Mr. Rose with and put it in the bottom of the ten-thousand-dollar casket her ashes would be buried in. I charged the burial casket to one of Billy Rose's credit cards. I also wrote a check on Billy Rose's account at Wells Fargo Bank and bought a twenty-five-hundred-dollar pair of gold hoop earrings for Marty's ears.

By the time I finished charging items to Billy Rose's credit cards and writing checks on his bank accounts, I'd spent more than fifty thousand dollars for Marty's funeral service, interment plot, and the catered repast. No one but Billy Rose and me would ever know I spent it, but he was the one I wanted to impress. I wanted him to know Mexican pussy wasn't as cheap as he and his father thought.

When I started to fold Marty's birth blanket to put in her casket, I remembered Shaun's blanket. That fuckin' philistine Rose, may he rot in hell, wouldn't allow Marty that one concession for Shaun's burial. He wouldn't let her put Shaun's birth blanket in the casket. I went through the box of things Marty had gotten from Mrs. Rose, found Shaun's blanket, and put it in the casket with her. The pure essence of his life from the fibers of his blanket would be mingled with hers.

I was in the crematorium with Marty when the undertaker pushed the cremation casket into the oven. Somewhere in the deep recess of my mind, where illogic lives, I expected her to cry out, "Get me out of here, you fool. I'm not dead." But it didn't happen and my fears quickly calmed. In my heart I knew her soul had already moved on.

For a while longer, there hung in the ambiance of the crematorium a syncopation of noises, heat reflux, and a wish it was all a very bad dream. Then silence settled softly around me. I was as calm as water in the eye of a storm. The oven cooled. The small bone fragments remaining were ground to ash with a pumice stone. Then the earthly remains of Martina Anna-Maria Sanchez de Valencia were deposited in a gold plated brass urn, which I would put in the casket, opposite the shotgun.

The memorial service was held Monday at one o'clock. Afterward, the mourners were feted with a repast of caviar and champagne, paid for by Billy Rose.

By two o'clock, everyone but Father Angelo and Miguel had left. Then Father Angelo excused himself. Miguel and I were alone.

He smiled and extended an envelope, which had been given to him for me. The handwriting on the outside startled me. The same person who wrote the note that had fallen out of the truck had written this message, too.

"This is something Enrique was working on," the message read.

I folded the envelope and stuck it in the jacket pocket of the suit I wore. *"Mañana,"* I told Miguel. "It will keep until tomorrow."

As we walked to the limo, which had been paid to wait for us by Billy Rose's American Express card, Miguel held my hand tight in his. The lawyer had yet to read the will, but it was clear to me I had inherited Miguel.

CHAPTER FORTY-ONE

The Tuesday after Marty's memorial service, I reported to work at my regular time and was met with disbelief from my fellow agents. Work was all I had and my plan was to work until I stopped grieving for all the things I didn't have. After working sixteen hours a day for the three remaining days of my workweek, I recognized the fallacy of my thinking. Grieving comes in cycles, like the tide. It rolls in, it rolls out. It slaps against the retaining wall, swells until it overflows the shoreline; then it gently recedes until the next time. But it never stops coming. At the end of that day, I requested and was granted a week of bereavement leave.

The first day of leave, I slept late and was awakened by a phone call from Mrs. Rose, who called to see if I had heard from Billy Rose. I said that I had, referring to the message he'd left on the answering machine, then realized he was one week overdue, but that wasn't what bothered me. What bothered me was just now remembering Marty saying Billy Rose came to see her the day she died. Why would he do that? Had he been back from Mexico all this time and hadn't acknowledged her death? Well, that was fine, too. Marty certainly wouldn't have appreciated him encroaching on my grief.

When Mrs. Rose hung up, I called Pete Ramirez at the Sheriff's Department and told him I'd broken up with Billy Rose and didn't know if the son of a bitch would become violent when he discovered the locks had been rekeyed.

"Call me if he does," Pete said. "I'd like an excuse to

kick his arrogant ass. I've seen him out having a good time without you, but you know, I didn't say anything."

Yes, I knew. The unofficial male code of silence.

"That's okay, Pete. There's been nothing between us for a couple of years, now. Not since Shaun . . . anyway, thanks. If he shows up, I'll call you before I shoot."

"Whichever," he said. "It'll be the same difference to me."

I dressed, stopped at the Circle K for a cup of coffee, asked Mrs. Kim if she'd seen Billy Rose. She said, "No." Then I went to Marty's house in Rio Rico to sort through her things, deciding what to keep and what to give away. It wasn't as hard a chore as I thought it would be. Over the past year, in anticipation of this, Marty had donated things she didn't use on a regular basis to the church rummage sale.

On the second day, the lawyer read Marty's will to her three beneficiaries: Miguel, Father Angelo, and me. As I expected, she left the house to Miguel. She left ten percent of her modest life insurance proceeds to Father Angelo's parish and the rest to a trust fund to take care of Miguel while he went to school.

"*Si,*" Miguel sadly smiled. "Learn English."

Marty owned a few Indian relics, which had been in her family for hundreds of years. She left those in my custody for her grandchildren, exposing her secret wish for me to have more children. To me Marty left an ornately carved chest, gilded in gold with a tiny golden key. I decided to open it when I was alone.

After dinner, after a swim, after a shower, I dressed for bed. Then I lit candles for Marty, Mr. Guzman, and Miguel's family. I pulled out the chest and sat cross-legged on the bed.

CAROLYN WILKERSON

I expected old letters from my father, maybe pictures, or some deep dark secrets Marty had promised to take to her grave. I never expected my very own collection of Shaun memorabilia. There were newspaper clippings, which reviewed his glory days as a high school athlete, and testimonials from teammates, coaches, and teachers who were shocked by the way he died. None had ever known him to use drugs.

There was a handprint he'd made for Mrs. Rose when he was in kindergarten and she'd given it to Marty. She also gave Marty the little white outfit and the blanket from his christening. My baby had worn that outfit, lain in the blanket, alive, squirming, plump, robust. And Marty gave them to me.

They were sealed in plastic. Carefully opening them, I brought the clothing to my face and the most wondrous baby smell tickled my nose. Shaun! Not his first essence, and not his final essence, but a lasting essence, now mine to have.

I breathed in Shaun deeply until I thought my lungs would explode. Tears filled my eyes. Pride swelled my heart. I had protected and loved Shaun when he was inside of me. Mrs. Rose and Father Angelo had done the same after he was born. Just maybe I had not failed him at all. All the testimonials from people who knew him best attested to his kind heart and good deeds. In the end, that is the only measure of one's life.

Upon internalizing this, my heart found peace with Shaun and released him to the care of the angels.

I quickly resealed the plastic bag so there would be more of Shaun to smell another time, another day when my heart needed a reason to beat.

Then I thought of Miguel. He was the same age as

HASTA MAÑANA

Shaun. Marty saw something innately good in him and took him on as her special project. Maybe it was her wish that he fill the void left by the son I'd never known. At least I believed it was. I would accept her challenge and stand by Miguel, fight for him, adopt him if necessary to keep him in the U.S. Most of all, I would love him like my own.

After placing the re-sealed plastic bag alongside the newspaper articles and handprint, cast in plaster of paris and painted green, I removed a small, untitled book with a locked strap from the chest. I found a small screwdriver in my jewelry case and removed the screws of the hasp.

The book was a journal kept by Shaun.

CHAPTER FORTY-TWO

GET OUT OF MY LIFE!!
Shaun posted this message on the first page of his journal. Then he proceeded to write a disclaimer. "This is a journal," he wrote, "not a diary. Girls keep diaries, and I'm not a fag. Of all the problems I have," he wrote, "that ain't one of them. But," he admitted, "saying ain't is."

The diary contained poetry and prose, simple notations, and near essay-length monologues about what he was feeling. He wrote about sports, girls, hopes, and dreams.

He started the journal during the last year of his life. A year in which he'd gone from boy to man in a lot of ways that could have been traumatic for him, but he tried to be upbeat and stay positive after each new discovery. He tried to understand. One of the traumas was finding out about his parentage. He wrote the following poem:

> My heart is bigger than my eyes.
> My mind is quicker than your lies.
> Let me share the secret.
> I'm not a baby who cries.

At the end of the poem he asked the question, "How long did they think they could keep something like that from me? I'm not a fucking idiot, and even if I were, I live with an alcoholic father who doesn't know what he's saying half the time."

Shaun wrote, "Dad likes me better than Billy. He calls

HASTA MAÑANA

Billy a 'pussy, just like your mother.' He said Billy is a 'marshmallow who would lie, steal, and cheat on those computer games he plays with but in real life he doesn't have the guts to kill a fly.' "

He wrote, "One day I told Billy I knew what he did for a living, that he had made more computerized drug deals than Mario Brothers did Donkey Kongs. I told him I knew what he kept in the extra gas tank, too, and he'd better get that shit out of my truck.

"Maybe Billy can't kill a fly, like Dad says, but he looked ready to kill me."

There were no more entries. Shaun was dead.

In the end there had been no secrets between us: my mother, my best friend, my son, and me. There had only been lies. Lies that maimed us, crippled us, turned us against each other, and killed us one by one.

I held the diary to my breast until the candles burned out. In the darkness I chanted my old chant: breath in, breath out. *Kill the bastard that killed Shaun.*

Two hours before dawn. Time to bury the last of my dead. Billy Rose: my best friend, my worst enemy.

I rose from the bed; pulled jeans and a shirt out of the dark cavern of my closet and put them on. Then I slipped my feet into my hiking boots and laced them up. Realizing it would be chilly in the desert where I was going, I reached back into the closet for a parka and touched the jacket I'd worn to Marty's funeral.

Then it made me remember something.

I reached into the pocket of the jacket and pulled out the envelope I'd stuffed in it almost a week before. I opened it and just as I'd smelled Shaun a few hours earlier, I smelled Enrique Guzman. He had thought of me in his last days, his last hours, maybe. I wanted to cry.

I pulled two sheets of paper from the envelope. The top sheet was a copy of my birth certificate; the empty space where my father's name should have been was highlighted. The second sheet was a list with forty-two names; forty-one had addresses and had been crossed out. In the margin, near the last name, he had penciled, *See Father Angelo. Name changed? Witness protection?*

I was speechless. Was number forty-two my father? How should I feel? What should I do? Did Father Angelo know where my father was?

"You have something more pressing to take care of," Marty said in my head. "Let it wait."

I didn't want to seem ungrateful for the countless hours Mr. Guzman must have spent on my behalf, but that chapter in my life had waited over thirty years. I put the paper in the chest with my other valuables and promised to take it out later when I could give it the consideration it deserved.

Now I had to find out what was in the auxiliary gas tank of Shaun's truck.

CHAPTER FORTY-THREE

My experience running out of gas in Mexico, and Shaun's notation in the journal both lent credence to one fact. The auxiliary tank on the truck did not hold gas. I didn't know how far I would have to drive to feel safe dismantling the auxiliary tank and inspecting it, but I didn't plan to run out of gas again. So when I got into the truck and checked the gauges, I also looked behind the seat to make sure the gas can was full.

It was not my conscious choice to go back to the canyon where I had first seen Mexican Joe, but my trip ended there at sunrise. Closed in on three sides, it gave me the privacy I needed for what I had to do.

I parked the truck across one of the deep ruts left from water running off during the spring rains. Then I was able to lie in the dirt depression under the truck and have plenty of elbowroom to loosen the nuts and bolts holding the tank. That part was relatively easy, and from the nicks and scratches on the metal, it was obvious it had been done before.

When I got the tank loose and hoisted it up on the bed of the truck, I wasn't surprised to see a heavy-duty padlock on the tank. I had brought a bolt cutter in anticipation of Billy Rose doing just that. It was inside the truck, under the seat where I had put it when I got in.

I went to the front of the truck, leaned over, grabbed the handle of the bolt cutter and pulled it to me, then felt something hit my boot. I looked down. It was a ring. I picked it up and looked at it. It was the same ring that had fallen from the ashtray the day the truck was returned and I had spilled the ashes. I slipped it on my middle finger and went back to the job of getting the tank open.

I cut the lock, removed the lid, and turned the tank upside down, but nothing fine and white spilled out. There was something hard in it though; it fell against the side of the tank when I shook it. I inspected the tank carefully and saw a section had been removed, then replaced with a welder's seam. After a few false starts and a couple of curses, I cut a slit in the lip of the tank. It was awkward going, but the bolt cutter was made of forged steel and I slowly cut out a section large enough for what was inside, a stack of CDs, to be removed.

Unfortunately all the noise I was making masked any sound Billy Rose may have made when he walked up behind me.

"You stupid bitch," he yelled from behind me. "Do you know what you've done?"

Although I instantly recognized the voice, he startled me. I dropped the bolt cutter on my foot.

And yes, I did know what I'd done. I'd let my relative seclusion lull me into a false sense of safety. Just as I had done the first time I came into this canyon and saw Mexican Joe. But I wasn't going to tell him that. "Jesus, Billy Rose," I said and turned to face him. He wore a loose-fitting jacket like agents wear when they carry guns. "You scared the shit out of me," I said. "Why'd you follow me out here?"

"Why the hell do you think? I want my fucking truck."

"Oh," I said, reached back and picked up the stack of CDs. "I suppose you want these, too. What's on them anyway, some kind of database?"

HASTA MAÑANA

I held up the CDs. "Is this what Shaun discovered in your truck? He was good with computers like you; I'll just bet he saw what's on them, too."

"I see you got my present," he said, smiling.

I followed his eyes to the hand that held up the CDs for his inspection. He was looking at the ring I'd just put on my finger. I remembered the message about a gift he'd left on the answering machine. I'd found the ring in the ashtray of the truck. Was it the gift?

Billy Rose's sinister laugh caused my brain to dig deeper. It took one second to remember I'd seen Mr. Guzman wearing this ring. It took another second for me to remember his fingers being chopped off, then another second for my mind to make the final association and me to gag and puke.

Billy Rose grabbed the CDs while I retched. "I'll take those," he said. "You're no good on the computer anyway."

"No, I'll take them," Mexican Joe said from the far side of the truck.

I couldn't believe he was there. He must have followed Billy Rose or me and stayed out of sight until he realized he'd stumbled onto the mother lode.

"I'm no good at computers either," he said. "But I know people who can break any computer code you can write, Billy Boy. They will have fun decoding these."

Mexican Joe walked around the truck and nodded to me. He held a gun on Billy Rose and took the CDs from his hand. The CDs probably contained enough information to put Billy Rose and several drug lords in prison for a long time.

"The black Navigator you asked me about was driven by Enrique," he said to me still looking at Billy Rose. "He was concerned about your safety and followed you until it became obvious he'd been spotted."

I know that SUV. He won't hurt you, Billy Rose had said. Did that also mean . . . ?

"Yes," Mexican Joe said. "He killed Enrique and cut off his fingers."

The ashes in the ashtray; he'd burned the evidence and left the ring as a gift for me. I looked at my hand. Instead of being repulsed, I would keep it.

Mexican Joe also looked at my hand.

"That's Enrique's ring," he said in disbelief. "How did you get it?"

He backed away as though he thought I had something to do with Mr. Guzman's murder and desecration.

In the instant he looked at the ring, Billy Rose pulled his gun out of his jacket and shot him.

Mexican Joe's arms flew up from the impact of the round and the gun fell from one hand and the CDs from the other. He fell backward to the ground. I ran to him while Billy Rose picked up the stack of CDs. I fell to my knees and screamed. "Did you have to kill him, too?"

"No," he said, "I didn't have to kill him. I wanted to kill him." He got in the truck and started it.

He backed up to where I still knelt over Mexican Joe. "This is what I do, Miriam," Billy Rose said. "This is why you've never had to want for anything."

His eyes looked wild and his voice was unusually high. "Are you coming with me or what?"

I put my head to Mexican Joe's chest, listened, and looked. The entry wound had left a small hole, and he looked to be asleep. I looked back at Billy Rose. A perverse cell of my being still connected me to him. An atom wanted to hope. Maybe we could still work this out. Maybe there was some reasonable explanation I had overlooked. Maybe.

HASTA MAÑANA

Maybe. Maybe. "I'm coming."

He leaned over the passenger seat and opened the door, while I went around the truck.

I picked up the CDs from the seat, held them in my hand, and sat down. Maybe they were programs for clients, maybe they were computer games, maybe they were porno films.

Billy Rose backed to the mouth of the canyon and stopped. He removed his jacket and walked back to where we'd stood. It took a few minutes to sweep away the tracks and walk backward, erasing the ones he made as he returned. It took even less for Marty in my head to say, " 'Maybe' isn't a word you trust. Unholster your gun, shove in a magazine of bullets."

Never put a bullet in your gun unless you intend to use it, we were taught at the Academy. I slipped the loaded gun under my leg.

As I watched Billy Rose throw his jacket in the bed of the truck, I adjusted my position in the seat so I would face him when he got into the cab, concealing the gun between the door and me.

"Well," he said. "That takes care of that. You'd never know we were here."

He sat for a minute looking in my eyes, into my soul. His face turned gray, he looked quickly away, then back. He knew. The hatred spurring me on this mission still burned hot in my heart. Still controlled my will. The cadence had never stopped, only the target.

"I'm starved," he announced, the cheeriness of his voice not matching the coldness in his eyes. "Let's get an early breakfast.

"And Miriam," he said. "Don't ever tell anyone what happened here."

"Okay," I said.

He looked surprised when I'd agreed. He asked, "Do I have to buy you something expensive to shut you up or will you give me your promise?"

"It won't bring him back or anything," I said, "but answer me this so we'll be done with it forever. Why did you have to kill Shaun?"

He shrugged his shoulders. "He was a wise ass kid."

I knew what I had to do. "My promise will do. No one will ever know what really happened here."

He started to drive away, then stopped short. Perhaps he read my mind when I thought, *One of us won't live to tell what happened; the other will take the secret to the grave.*

Perhaps this was what he'd come to do and he'd just now garnered the nerve to do it. But when he turned and looked at me, Billy Rose's face looked like it did the time he had to put his dog, Boris, down.

He exhaled loudly and said, "You win, Miriam. You finally fuckin' win. You made me stop loving you, now you're more trouble to me than you're worth."

He reached for his gun.

I shot him through the heart.

I grabbed my belongings and the CDs, jumped from the truck, and started the long walk home.

When I was a safe distance, I turned, aimed at the gas tank, and fired again.

Shaun's red truck exploded into flames.

CHAPTER FORTY-FOUR

Officer Pete Ramirez of the Pima County Sheriff's Department looked at me doubtfully. "I know you as well as anyone around here, Miriam, and I want to believe what you're telling me, but there's just no evidence to prove a homicide occurred out there where you said."

I could tell Pete wanted to believe me, but he wasn't going to lose any sleep over it either way. When I'd walked into his office to report the crime, he'd said, "What we're talking about here is Billy Rose and a drug smuggler, right? Both probably deserved what they got."

But I had insisted. So the police scoured the canyon and the most they would concede was that a section of the sand looked like it might be slightly off-color from the adjacent sand.

"Are you sure you sent us to the right place?"

"I'm positive. I was sure the Forestry Service would see the smoke and go investigate right away. I couldn't carry the man back here; burning the truck was the quickest way I knew to get help."

"I'll call them," he said.

Five minutes later, Pete returned. "They did have a report of smoke."

"Did they investigate?"

"What do you think? After half the forests in Central America just finished burning, you know the Forestry Service investigated smoke. But all they found was some charred residue. They wrote it up as campers, but you and I know something as large as a burned vehicle would leave enough charred residue to resemble a barn fire, not a campfire.

"You might want to report the truck stolen, though, just in case you have to collect from your insurance company later on."

"It was already reported stolen in Mexico," I said, "by the owner."

"Miriam," Pete said as he walked me to the door. "Are you sure the other man *wasn't* dead?"

"I'm positive he wasn't dead. I screamed like he was dead so Billy Rose wouldn't shoot again, but when I put my head to his chest, I felt his breath on my face. Then he told me, 'Go.' "

"Well, I was just thinking," Pete said. "If this man was DEA like you said, and he showed up out of nowhere, there may have been someone else out there in 'nowhere,' who got help. It took you a long time to hike back here. If the government saw fit, they could sweep that canyon so clean you wouldn't find guano in those bat caves.

"Don't sweat it," Pete said.

That's what Marty said inside my head, the instant remorse clutched my heart. "Don't sweat it, Baby. He got what he paid for."

"I'm not sweating it, Pete. Billy Rose drew down on me first."

"I don't give a shit about him," Pete blasted back at me. "I was talking about the other guy. You probably saved his life."

I smiled.

Of course I saved Mexican Joe's life.

Marty said I would.

ABOUT THE AUTHOR

Carolyn Wilkerson graduated from Livingstone College and received a doctorate degree from Rutgers, the State University of New Jersey. She was a closet writer for the many years while she pursued a career and raised a son, who grew up to be a federal agent.

Carolyn lives in North Carolina and New Jersey, where she is writing another Miriam Valencia novel.